Beach House Beauty

A Curvy Girl Romance

Nichole Rose

Contents

Dedication

To the man I idolized – I still miss you.

About the Book

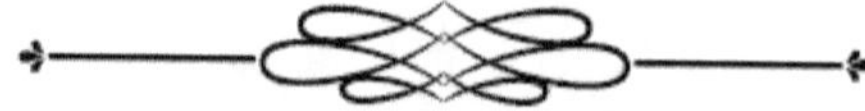

Can an orphaned heiress find forever with her father's best friend, or will a deadly secret destroy them both?

Raven Calloway

Three months ago, my father died.

In the blink of an eye, my whole life changed.

I'm homeless, penniless, and adrift.

Until my father's best friend, Rhys Flannery, offers me a place to stay.

He grounds me in ways I never expected.

Sets me on fire in ways I've only dreamed about.

But he's keeping secrets that threaten to destroy us both.

How do I trust him with my heart when he's the only one capable of shattering it?

Rhys Flannery

Three months ago, my best friend was murdered.

When his daughter shows up on my doorstep, I can't turn her away.

She's been my obsession since the day I met her.

But she doesn't know the secrets I'm keeping.

Telling her what I know will destroy her entire world.

Keeping the truth from her may destroy us.

I refuse to let that happen.

I will protect her, even if I have to destroy myself to do it.

If you enjoy safe instalove reads featuring growly older men, strong BBW heroines, and sizzling romance, you'll love Raven and Rhys! As always, Nichole Rose books come with a sticky-sweet and guaranteed HEA.

Prologue

RHYS

THREE YEARS AGO

"Well, look what the cat dragged in," Brantley Calloway says as I step out onto his back patio. He lifts a beer in mock salute, a shit-eating grin on his face. Dressed in gray chino shorts and a red polo, he's the picture of modish relaxation. A rarity for him. He's usually in five-thousand-dollar suits and expensive Italian leather shoes, lines of stress etched around his blue eyes. "I was beginning to think you stood us up."

"Got held up at work," I say, propping a shoulder up against the glass door as I scan the backyard. There are two dozen people scattered around the elegant pool, all dressed in equally elegant swimwear, all chatting and laughing. Aside from Brant's wife, Marnie, and his business partner, Jack Hale, I don't know any of them. I'm not surprised. Brant and I are from two different worlds.

My family is wealthy, but not like this. Brant is a whole different level of affluent. He lives in a sprawling eleven-thousand square-foot mansion on Lake Washington. The backyard is an oasis of indulgent luxury, with colorful gardens, an Olympic-sized pool carved from natural rock, tennis courts, a pool house, a guest house, and a killer view of the lake.

I paid a king's ransom for a two-story Craftsman in West Seattle twelve years ago. It's small, but it's mine. It's worth twice what I paid for it now, but I'm not giving it up easy. I'm a homicide detective. The pay is garbage. Luckily, I've made some good investments over the years, and working security for Brant on days off has been a nice little bonus. I'm not hurting for cash. I'm not in a hurry to spend it either. I prefer to live modestly and make my own way in life.

I'm guessing everyone else at this little barbeque throws money around like it's nothing. Brant keeps expensive company. He doesn't like any of them much, at least not that I can tell. They seem to be more Marnie's friends than his. In the year I've worked for him, he's always kept them at a polite distance. He welcomes them into his home, but he doesn't trust them. He doesn't seem to trust much of anyone but me and Jack.

The only people in the world with more trust issues than cops are billionaires. Maybe that's why Brant and I get along so well. We're both suspicious of everyone under the sun.

"Working another case?" he asks, flipping steaks on the grill.

"Always," I grunt in response. We had a triple homicide two days ago. I've been working my ass off trying to run the suspect to ground. He finally turned himself in at midnight last night. Confessed everything. "Where's the beer?"

Brant points the spatula toward the fridge behind him.

I push away from the door, headed in that direction. "You're burning the meat," I observe, peeking in at the charred steaks on my way past. "Didn't anyone ever teach you how to grill a steak?"

"Didn't anyone ever teach you not to shit talk the man cooking your food and signing your checks?" he retorts, side-eyeing me. "Raven won't eat it if it's still mooing at her."

"She's here?" I ask with interest, reaching into the outdoor fridge for a beer. Since I met him, Brantley has talked nonstop about his daughter, but I've never set eyes on the kid. She lives in New York with her mom and has been busy with school. Brant usually flies back to New York once a month to spend time with her instead of dragging her across the country.

He's a good man. Most men in his position couldn't give two shits about family. It's all about the bottom dollar. That isn't Brant. His family comes first, even if it means business takes a backseat. Hell, he moved his entire company across the country for Marnie when he married her four years ago. He wanted her happy, and Seattle was her home.

"Yeah, she'll be here for a few weeks before she heads to Boston," he says. "She wants time to get familiar with the city before classes start."

Ah, shit. I forgot Raven graduated last month. She starts college at Berklee this fall. She's a voice major. Brant was proud as hell when she got accepted early admission. He says she sings like an angel. Even Marnie says she's good. That's a ringing endorsement from a woman who doesn't leave her own world often enough to notice anyone else exists most of the time.

Marnie isn't a bad woman. She's just self-absorbed and shallow. Then again, when you're the heiress to a literal gold mine, I guess you can be. Her family owns the oldest mining company left in the United States. Owned. Her parents died when she was younger, leaving everything to her. But Brant is crazy about her, and she's crazy about Brant, so I mind the business that pays me.

I'm curious about Raven, though. From the way Brant talks about her, she's the exact opposite of her stepmother. There isn't a shallow or self-absorbed bone in her body. Her life revolves around music and volunteering for a music program in NYC. She graduated at the top of her class, never gets into trouble, and is an all-around good girl.

Either she's the most well-adjusted billionaire's kid on the planet, or she's one hell of an actress. Call me cynical, but my money is on the latter. No one grows up in the lap of luxury without a few demons. When you can have whatever you want, and the whole world caters to your every whim, you leave a few skeletons in your wake. I've seen it far too often to believe any different.

This city is overrun with spoiled rich kids who think the rules don't apply to them. I'll bet my left nut Raven's the same way. She may have Brant fooled, but he hasn't spent the last fifteen years in uniform. I was cleaning up the messes of rich kids long before I started working homicide. Hell, I grew up with the blood of one running through my veins. My mother has been a spoiled brat her whole life. Everyone in her vicinity has suffered for it, my baby sister the most.

I don't tell Brant any of that, though. His kid is his business.

"She should be down soon," Brant says as I pop the top on my bottle and take a pull. "She and Marnie had a...disagreement about her swimsuit." His expression tightens, displeasure pulling his lips down at the corners. "I had to intervene."

My gaze flickers to Marnie. I'm not sure how she has a leg to stand on regarding what Raven wears when she's dressed like she is. Her suit consists of a few tiny gold triangles held together by several even smaller strings. It leaves nothing to the imagination. Not that she seems to mind how every man in attendance looks at her. Jack's ogling her tits so hard I'm surprised he hasn't given himself an aneurysm. Marnie's relishing in the attention where she holds court beside the pool. But that's not my business either, so I keep my mouth shut and take another drink.

"I'm taking Raven out on the boat tomorrow. Are you free?" Brant asks.

"Where are you headed?"

"She wants to see the whales." He smiles indulgently. "I figured I'd take her on a cruise around the islands, see if we can't find a pod for her. Marnie has a meeting, so it'll just be the two of us."

I open my mouth to agree, only for movement at the door to catch my attention. A tall, raven-haired beauty steps outside, her arms wrapped around her curvy body, her cheeks stained pink.

My breath gets lodged in my throat, every thought in my head vanishing. Christ Almighty. She has legs for days. And curves sweet enough to make my cock ache. Her all-black, two-piece suit is modest compared to what most women here are wearing, but it looks indecent on her full figure anyway. Her breasts nearly spill from the scalloped top, the creamy swells making my mouth water. The high waist leaves a tantalizing strip of her pale stomach visible. It's clear she's not entirely comfortable in the suit, but she looks gorgeous.

She's beautiful in a timeless way, fresh-faced and innocent. Her big blue eyes and pouty lips are straight out of the old black and white movies my sister loves. She's captivating, enchanting. I can't pull my eyes away from her. Unlike most of the women here, she isn't reed thin but big and beautiful. Her stomach isn't flat but round, her hips and thighs wide. She's the kind of woman you sink into and take your time with. The kind you ride bare just because you can't fucking resist.

The blood in my veins heats like metal in a forge at the thought, desire screaming through me. I don't know who she is, but I decide immediately that she will be mine. There is no other option. It's been years since I was last with anyone. Hell, it's been months since I got myself off. But I need this woman beneath me more than I need my next breath. I need to know what she looks like with those dark curls spread across my bed and those thick thighs wrapped around my head.

I take a step in her direction.

"There she is," Brant says.

I whip my head in his direction, unsure what he's talking about or who. Marnie? His kid? His boat? I stopped listening as soon as the mystery woman appeared on the patio.

"Come here, baby girl," he calls. "I want you to meet someone."

My mystery girl turns toward us in slow motion, a sweet smile overtaking her face.

Ah, fuck.

My stomach knots up, my balls churning.

There's no way this is his kid. This woman isn't a girl or anything remotely close to it. She's a full-fledged goddess sent down from Mount Olympus.

"Hi, dad," she says, moving in our direction. Her hips sway with every step. And that voice. Christ. If she sings half as sweet as she speaks, she really does sing like a fucking angel.

I tip my beer back, draining the bottle.

Her gaze shifts to me as Brant gives her a one-armed hug. Those big blue eyes widen almost comically when they lock on my face, her pouty lips parting slightly. Jesus Christ. I want to slip my dick between them while she stares at me like that.

"Raven, this is Rhys Flannery," Brant says as we stare at each other in complete silence. "Rhys, this is my baby girl, Raven."

"Hi, Rhys," she whispers, looking up at me through the longest lashes I've ever seen. A blush stains her cheeks, her tits shuddering as she says my name. "It's really nice to meet you."

Brant moves back to the grill.

"Raven," I growl, cursing God and all His saints for putting this sweet little thing in front of me and making her utterly untouchable at the same time. I may be an asshole, but there are some lines even I won't cross. She's my best friend's daughter, the light of his life. I can't—won't—put my hands on her. But God, I want to.

"Um, my dad says you're a detective? That must be interesting," she says, her gaze eating me up. I don't have to ask to know she likes what she sees. It's written all over her face. She wears the truth like she does her innocence, right there for the whole world to see.

Brant hasn't seen it yet. He's busy flipping steaks. But any minute now, he's going to look up again. He's going to see how she's looking at me, and he's going to know that his baby girl has a thing for me. I have to shut it down now. I owe him that much.

Forgive me, songbird, I think regretfully, wishing like hell she was anyone else. If she were, I'd answer any question she wanted to ask, tell her anything she wanted to know. But she's Brant's kid. That's a line you don't cross.

"I am," I say, arranging my face into a disapproving frown. "But I don't think your dad would appreciate you asking about my job, Raven. You're way too young to know about the kind of shit people in this world do to one another."

Her face falls, hurt channeling through her expressive eyes.

"I need another beer," I mutter, feeling like the world's biggest asshole. But I don't take back the harsh words.

For her sake, I can't.

Chapter One

RHYS

PRESENT DAY

"You should come home," I growl into the phone, glaring out my kitchen window. Rain sheets from the sky, turning Friday Harbor into a hazy blob. Boats bob up and down in the water to the north, bouncing on their moorings. The usual, steady flow of traffic in the picturesque island town has ground to a halt. Everyone is inside, trying to wait out the storm.

They'll be waiting a while. The storm isn't expected to blow over until tomorrow at the earliest. Hopefully, that'll keep the tourists off the island for one day. They're the lifeblood of this place, but they've been swarming the island in droves. It's only June. We still have four full months of the season to go.

A man can only take so much. And I've had about all I can stand for the week. My people skills have never been great.

They're even worse when drunk tourists are involved. They drive me nuts. Sue me.

"Rhys," Cassia cries into the phone. "I'm not coming back to Washington. Will you stop saying that?"

"No," I mutter, my scowl deepening. Even in the window, deep grooves appear on my forehead, making my displeasure evident. I'm irritable as all hell. It's my permanent state.

Four months ago, my baby sister went on a girl's trip to Lake Tahoe for Valentine's Day, where she met, fell in love with, and married Cord Decker in a whirlwind romance. I don't like it. Sure, he's head over heels in love with her. Sure, I like him well enough. Sure, he treats her like a queen. But she's my baby sister. I want her back in Washington, where I can keep an eye on her. God knows she needs it.

Trouble has a way of finding Cassia. Or rather, Cassia has a way of finding trouble. Case in point: today's shitshow. She caught a field on fire, trying to teach herself how to build a bonfire for one of her books. Cord and his ranch hands were able to put it out before it did too much damage, but Christ Almighty. My sister is a menace. Cord should know better than to leave her to her own devices. She has terrible ideas.

"This is my home now," she says with a huff. "I'm not coming back to Washington, Rhys."

"Put Cord on the phone."

"Why?" she asks, her tone rife with suspicion.

"I want to talk to him."

"About what?"

"Stuff."

"What stuff?"

"Just put him on the phone, Cassia," I say, cracking a rare smile.

"Uh, no. It's not his fault I'm good at setting things on fire," she says.

"Good?" I quirk a brow, not sure how she reached that conclusion. "You set the field on fire, Cass."

"Exactly. If I were bad at it, I wouldn't have been able to start one at all, don't you think?" she asks, completely serious.

"You..." Well, hell. She might have a point there. "Regardless of the semantics," I say, moving away from the window as a clap of thunder strikes in the distance, rattling the pane of glass. "Tell your husband I'll kill him if anything happens to you."

Three months ago, I lost my best friend. I'll be damned if I lose my baby sister too. Losing Brantley still has me fucked up in the worst way. The guilt is unbearable, but the burden is mine to carry anyway.

What I did...well, hell has a special place for people like me. But I can't take it back. I'm not sure I even regret it. If he were here, I'm pretty damn confident he'd have made the same choice I did. Or maybe he wouldn't have. I don't know. Turns out, I didn't know a lot of things.

Brantley Calloway had secrets. A lot of them. And I never had a clue.

I ate at his table, fished on his boat...drank his beer. He's the reason I'm living on the island now. Without his support, I'd still be up to my ears in open homicide cases in Seattle. Instead, I'm one of two detectives in San Juan County. I spend the majority of my time investigating the bullshit that comes with tourism—assaults, robberies, theft. My job is golden compared to what it used to be.

Working homicide wears you down. It's sixteen-hour shifts, six and seven days a week. There's an endless parade of names and faces forever burned into my mind. None died easy. Most don't rest easy either. Justice doesn't bring back the dead or heal broken hearts. It never made much of a dent in the stack of open files on my desk, either.

I thought I had left all that behind. And then Marnie called me three months ago. She was hysterical, screaming that Brant was dead. My neatly ordered existence blew up in my face right then and there. I did what I had to do to protect the people who matter, but I damned myself in the process.

There are some things Raven never needs to know.

I'll take those secrets to my grave to protect her. There isn't a lot I won't do for her.

When we met three years ago, she knocked me flat on my ass with those big blue eyes. When she isn't singing, she's the sweetest little lamb, so shy and quiet. But as soon as she opens that mouth, she turns into a siren, alluring and confident. The combination fascinates me. But she's Brantley's kid, so I've spent the last three years avoiding the hell out of her. I thought eventually I'd forget about her. That never happened. But I managed to keep from occupying the same space as her for three fucking years. I managed to keep my hands to myself.

Right up until Brant died.

As soon as I picked her up from the airport, I hugged her, and it was over for me. I didn't leave her side the whole time she was here for the funeral. I couldn't. The guilt tore me apart. Seeing her so fucking sad broke my heart. She deserves answers about what happened to her father, but I have none to give her. None that won't tear her world apart, anyway. She idolized her dad. Knowing what I know won't help her sleep easy. All it'll do is destroy the image she has of the man who worshipped the ground she walked on.

My gaze drifts to the file spread across my kitchen table, my mind working through the facts for the thousandth time. None of it makes sense, yet it's all there in black and white. I have more questions than answers, and the deeper I look, the more I wish I'd left it the fuck alone.

Brantley Calloway was in bed with the mob. His money was dirty. His company was dirty. *He* was dirty.

And his pregnant wife killed him.

"Rhys!" Cassia cries. "Are you even listening to me?"

"Yes, I'm listening to you," I say, shaking my head to clear it.

"Then what did I say?" she demands to know.

I didn't hear a word she said, but Cassia is easy to figure out. "You're bitching at me about threatening to kill your man," I say, ticking each point off on my fingers. "He's the love of your life and my new brother-in-law. I need to stop threatening to kill him all the time. It makes you sad. You want the world to be full of rainbows and butterflies and everyone you love to hold hands and sing kumbaya around the campfire."

"I did not say that," she says, laughing. "You are so full of it."

"I was paraphrasing. And you know it's true anyway."

"Whatever," she huffs. "I do not want you to hold hands with Cord." Her soft laughter floats down the line again. "But maybe you can stop threatening to kill him so much? You've made your point already. He's not going anywhere."

"I deal with drunk tourists who like to fight all day long, Cassia. Threatening him is the only joy left in my life."

"You mean since your friend died."

I growl at her, my brows pulling together in a deep scowl even though she can't see me. "We aren't talking about that."

"Why not?"

"Cassia." I pinch the bridge of my nose. "Don't you have a husband to terrorize? Or a book to write? Or a runaway bull to hunt down?"

"No. I mean, yes, probably. But you never talk about your stuff," she complains. "You just act all 'me man, me feel no pain' about it. It's lame. You can talk to me, you know."

"Me man, me feel no pain?" I repeat, chuckling despite myself. I love my sister. She's completely crazy, and Cord will have his hands full for the rest of his life, but she's also the best person I know. Our mother put her through hell growing up, but she never let it stop her from being her. She's wild and messy and has no filter. But she loves fiercely and never apologizes for it.

"You know what I mean. You just keep it all to yourself and never talk about it. I worry about you, Rhys," she says, her voice soft. "Especially with you out on the island by yourself."

"I'm fine, Cassia. I'm dealing with it."

"How?"

"By dealing with it."

She growls at me.

"I'm not talking to you about my job. You don't need to know anything about murders and murderers or any of the fucked-up shit that goes on in this world," I say, my tone firm as I pace around the kitchen. The whole back wall of the house looks out over the water, flooding the house with natural light when it's sunny out. Thanks to the storm, shadows overtake the kitchen now, creeping into the corners. They fit my mood. "You need to write your books and keep pouring light into the world. I'll deal with the dark."

"You're working his case?"

There is no case to work. Seattle PD is chasing a carefully crafted lie.

"Not officially."

"But you're working it."

"Yes," I sigh instead of telling her the ugly truth. She doesn't need to know the lies I've told and the crimes I've committed. "I'm working it."

"Okay," Cassia says and then drops the subject. "Are you going to see Lindee and your dad soon?"

"Probably not. They're in Cancun." Now that my dad is retired, he and my stepmom spend most of their time traveling. They come home for holidays and major events but otherwise live like nomads. They love it.

"Well, tell her to give you a big hug from me next time you see her," Cassia demands. She and I don't share a dad, but my parents love her. I think they would have adopted her themselves if they could have done it. It certainly would have been better for Cassia than growing up under our mother's thumb.

I have as little to do with our mother as possible. She may have given me life, but she didn't raise me. My dad and my stepmom did. She's never been a mother to me. She's never cared about anyone but herself. My loyalties lie with Cassia. She didn't have a choice in how she was raised. Our mother did. She was mentally and emotionally abusive to Cassia for most of her life. I fucking *hate* that I didn't know sooner. I hate that I wasn't there to protect her. I'll never forgive our mother for the shit she put Cassia through or for the scars and insecurities Cassia now carries. She deserved better. She still does.

Thank God my stepmom sees it. It's taken Cassia a long time to open up to her, but my stepmom is determined to make sure Cassia knows that she's loved and that she's a welcome and wanted part of our family. She may not belong to my dad and Lindee, but she's my sister. As far as they're concerned, that makes her family for life.

"I will," I promise Cassia, pulling out a chair at the long farm table that stretches the length of the back wall.

"Call you later," she says. "Love you, Rhys."

"I love you too, baby sister. Behave."

Cassia laughs, which I take to mean she intends to ignore that order and then hangs up. I drop my phone on the table beside me and then ease myself down into the chair. For a long moment, I just run my eyes over the various pieces of information spread across the tabletop, trying to make sense of it.

"Who the fuck were you?" I mutter, picking up a photo of Brant. He's on my fishing boat, a beer in one hand, a smile on his face, his skin bronzed from the sun. He was a handsome SOB, I'll give him that, with light hair, blue eyes, and that all-American look that drove women crazy. They were constantly hitting on the bastard. Didn't care that he was in love with his wife. Didn't care that he had a kid their age. Women flocked to him.

I set the picture aside and pick up one of him and Raven. She has his eyes and his height. I never met her mom—she and Brant were over before they ever began—but I'm guessing Raven got the rest of her looks from her. She's five-ten or five-eleven but still looks short next to Brant. Hell, she looks short next to me too. I'm six-five.

My cock stiffens in my pants, stirring as I stare at the photo of her. As I remember the feel of her in my arms, her soft curves pressed to my body, her vanilla scent wreaking havoc on my system.

"Jesus Christ," I growl, dropping the photo to scrub a hand down my face. If I weren't already going to hell, lusting after my best friend's daughter while she cried in my arms would undoubtedly do it. I couldn't help it, though. Trying to purge her from my mind is impossible. I've been trying for three years. She's stuck like a song playing on repeat. The lyrics play on no matter how often I try to focus on something else.

Another clap of thunder rattles the windowpanes. It fades to a soft tap echoing through the house. I pick up another photo, determined to put Raven out of my head and try to figure out how deep Brant's connection to the mob goes. I need answers, if for no other reason than to unravel this fucking mess and find a way out of it.

I'm juggling a house of cards here. But I can't let it fall. Raven has no one left. Her mom died right before her nineteenth birthday. Her dad is gone now. The only family she has left is the sibling growing in her stepmom's belly. If the truth gets out about Brant, they'll lose everything. Wasn't that Marnie's threat?

I'll tell the world who he really was. Will he still be a hero to her then, Rhys? Will you?

The soft tap echoes through the house again. It takes a minute to realize it's not thunder at all.

Someone is knocking on my front door.

I toss the photo down and stride that way. Storms can be deadly on the island, especially to unsuspecting tourists. They explore a little too far and get caught in dangerously precarious positions. They slip and fall, plunging into water frigid enough to jolt the human body into cold shock or rile the wild animals who call this island and surrounding waters home. Accidents are a fact of life around here, especially on days like today. And I'm a certified diver. I get called on frequently to assist.

I throw the front door open, prepared for anything.

Except for the woman standing on my doorstep.

"Raven?"

Water drips from the ends of the dark hair plastered to her face. She's so pale; her ivory skin is nearly translucent. Every inch of her clothing is soaked through, and she's trembling, her lips tinged blue. Her hands, clutched tightly around a single rolling suitcase, are stark white.

"H-h-hi," she says through chattering teeth. Her attempt at a smile trembles and falls before it ever fully forms. She sways on her feet, shivering uncontrollably.

"Jesus Christ," I growl, leaping forward to grab her before she plummets to the ground at my feet. I wrap an arm around her waist, hauling her up against me. Her skin is ice cold, water still sluicing from her curvy body. "Are you trying to get yourself killed out there?"

"I-I-I..." She gives up trying to explain when she can't get the words out through her chattering teeth and shivering body. She's too fucking cold, too pale.

My heart pounds, fear for her coursing through me with every heavy beat. I scoop her up, suitcase and all, and carry her into the house, kicking the door closed behind me. Her suitcase falls to the tile floor with a thud. I step over it, charging toward the bedroom as fury churns through me.

What the hell was she doing out there?

Did she walk all the way here from the ferry terminal?

It may be June, but the temperature is in the low fifties, and it's a good twenty-minute walk here on a good day. Today is the exact-fucking-opposite of a good day. The rain is frigid. It's been hailing on and off for hours.

"W-w-w-what?"

"Warming you up," I growl, answering her question before she can finish it. I carry her into the primary suite and then straight through to the bathroom. As soon as we're over the threshold, I set her on the vanity and grab a fluffy black bath towel. "Your skin is like ice. We need to get you out of these clothes and get you into something warm and dry."

Her teeth chatter again.

I wrap the towel around her, chafing her arms with it to sop up as much excess water from her skin as I can. She tries to help but shakes too hard to be helpful. I set my jaw, clenching my teeth to keep from snarling like a wild beast.

The cop in me is ready to demand answers. Raven is smart. Too smart to pull a stunt like this. The overprotective man who thinks about her endlessly wants to cuddle her close and fix whatever drove her here. And the possessive, autocratic asshole wants to spank her perfect ass. I'm all three at once, warring for control.

She's trembling too hard to help me strip her wet clothes from her body. I try like hell not to look at her soft curves, and the tantalizing peeks of porcelain skin beneath my rough hands, but I can't help but see them. I can't help but see her.

Brantley, you son of a bitch. You're supposed to be here. You're supposed to stop this.

Except...he's not. He can't.

At this point, I'm not even sure heaven itself could stop me from claiming this little songbird as my own. God help us both; I'm not sure anything can.

Chapter Two

RAVEN

"Don't move," Rhys growls.

I swallow hard at the thunderous scowl etched into his handsome face, trying to burrow deeper into my own naked embrace as shivers wrack my body.

How did I get here? I wonder, watching him as he storms from the bathroom. The muscles in his upper arms and back bunch and coil, shifting as he turns slightly to fit his broad frame through the door. I'm naked and soaking wet, drenched in tears and shame. Meanwhile, he looks like he should be throwing tires down a football field instead of investigating violent crimes.

He might be the biggest man I've ever met. He's undoubtedly the hottest...and the grumpiest. I'm pretty sure his forest green eyes see right through me. They pick the dirty thoughts out of my head as if I spoke them aloud. It's impossible to look at him and not think them, though. He's so damn sexy to me, like a storybook hero.

If, you know, storybook heroes were cranky giants with windswept dark hair, uneven lips, bold tattoos, and skin permanently bronzed from the sun. And if they also happened to star in every dirty dream you have and be your deceased father's best friend and personal security guard. I don't think there are many storybook heroes like him.

I also don't think he's particularly happy to see me. Not that I blame him since I just showed up unannounced on his doorstep with a suitcase. I didn't intend to come here at all, but my dad always told me to trust Rhys.

He's a good man, poppet. One of the best I've ever met. If you're ever in trouble, you find him, you hear me? You find Rhys. He'll protect you.

I think I'm in trouble now.

My whole world is falling apart at the seams. I have no home. No family. No money. Nothing.

Right before my nineteenth birthday, my mom died in a car accident. I didn't think I was going to survive it, but I had my dad to help me through it. Now, he's gone too. Three months ago, he was killed in a robbery gone wrong. Whoever broke in didn't expect to find him at home. They murdered him and ransacked the house. Seattle Police Department still has no leads.

They're dragging their feet while my world slowly collapses.

Little by little, my stepmom chipped away at everything I had left. She canceled my credit cards first, saying it was time I learned how to be responsible for myself. Then she canceled my tuition payment for my final year at Berklee; only she waited until the last minute to tell me. It's too late to apply for scholarships for next year. I won't graduate.

She also waited until I flew home today to tell me I couldn't stay with her this summer. I've spent every summer with my dad since my mom died. I have nowhere else to go. I always knew she didn't like me much, but I never knew how much she hated me until I landed at Sea-Tac, and she dropped the bomb on me. She couldn't even be bothered to do it in person.

I just want my dad back.

"Are you crying?" Rhys growls.

I jump, my gaze flying upward.

He's standing in the doorway, a pile of clothes in his arms, a look of horror on his face. It's the same way he looked at me when I cried the day he picked me up from the airport three months ago. The day after my dad died.

This bristling, scowling giant was so kind to me then. I don't remember much from that week, but I remember him. He was a bright spot in the dark, my port in the storm. He just walked right up to me at the airport, wrapped his arms around me, and promised me I would be okay.

I hadn't cried until that moment. It didn't feel real until then. But in his arms, the tears finally came. I sobbed while he held me, not caring that everyone passing by could see me. Not caring that they were probably taking pictures. If they did, I never saw them. Rhys wrapped me up in his arms and shut out the entire world.

All week, his presence kept the world at bay. He took care of everything while I drifted through the whole awful affair in a fog of grief. I ate because he made sure I did. I slept for the same reason. I survived because he was beside me, lending me his strength. I don't remember the details. I couldn't tell you the first thing about the service. I don't know who spoke. Who shook my hand. Who hugged me or offered their condolences. I don't know who was kind to me or who whispered behind my back. All I remember is Rhys sitting beside me the whole time, his rough hand clasped tightly around mine.

"Why are you crying, Raven? What the fuck happened?" He grows before my eyes, bigger, fierce. *Dangerous*, my mind whispers. "Did someone hurt you?"

Only my heart, I want to say. The only thing that emerges from my lips is a pitiful, wretched sob. I clamp a hand over my mouth to stifle the sound, embarrassed that I'm crying in front of him again. I did enough of that three months ago.

"Fuck," he swears, crossing to me in two steps. His strong arms close around me.

I let him drag me up against his chest. I'm too damned cold and miserable to resist. I've missed him. More than I want to admit. More than I think he'd like to know. Rhys doesn't like me much. I think I'm an obligation to him, someone he pities.

To me, he's the standard by which I've measured every man since I was eighteen and met him for the first time. None ever competed. None ever compared. They weren't handsome enough or strong enough, or brave enough. They didn't scowl enough or growl enough. Their eyes weren't the right shade of forest green.

They didn't make me ache.

Rhys does. He has for three long years. He doesn't know it, but I've been in love with him since I first set eyes on him. The only time we ever met before my dad died, he took one look at me and seemed to hate me on sight. It wasn't like that for me. I took one look at him and felt like I was staring at the sun. He blazed so brightly that he blinded me, leaving behind a permanent, lasting image of himself.

I came alive that day in ways I never was before. For the first time, I understood the desire I'd only ever experienced through song. I'd sung about the piercing ache so many times, but I never truly understood it until then. How deep it went, how much it changed you. How completely it eclipsed *everything*.

And then my dad introduced him, and I realized he was unattainable, something forever out of my reach. To him, I would never be anything but his best friend's annoying kid, someone he didn't even want to converse with, let alone see as a woman.

Even if he *had* seen me that way, he was off-limits. My dad would have lost his mind.

"I'm s-s-sorry," I sob, clinging to him with both hands. "I d-d-didn't h-have anyw-where else to g-g-go."

"Shh, songbird," he whispers, lifting me into his arms. "It's okay. I've got you."

I burrow into him, desperate to believe him, if only for a moment. Desperate to believe, if only for a moment, that he's mine and I'm not wholly and utterly alone in this world.

"Talk to me, Raven," Rhys says. I'm on his lap, a thick quilt wrapped around me. A fire roars in the fireplace, piping heat into the living room. His place is beautiful. The entire back wall is glass, looking out over the water. The storm still blows fiercely outside. Waves batter the shore like the rain hammering the metal roof. It's oddly soothing. His furniture is rustic and comfortable. *Warm.*

I stopped shivering half an hour ago. I stopped crying not long after that. He hasn't pushed, though. He's been patiently waiting me out. It's odd. I don't think he's an exceptionally patient person at all. My dad always said he was an impatient, bossy bastard. But he's patient with me. At least he was at my dad's funeral and has been again today.

It's not what I expected.

"Marnie cut me off," I whisper woodenly.

"What the fuck?" he growls.

"She said my dad coddled me too much." Maybe she's right. I'm almost twenty-two, and I have no job and no home of my own. I have what's in the bank from when my mom died, but that's not much. Unlike my dad, my mom wasn't rich. She lived her life one day at a time. Her life wasn't glamorous, but she loved every minute of it.

She and my dad got along surprisingly well. I was a surprise baby, the product of a summer fling. She was a lounge singer. He was a twenty-year-old with big dreams. They hit it off immediately. When I showed up nine months later, he was already making a name for himself. He and my mom agreed that she'd keep custody of me, and he'd be allowed to see me whenever he wanted. He was always a part of my life. Their brief affair fizzled quickly, but they were always friends. They were always family. For years, it was just the three of us.

At least until my dad met Marnie when I was sixteen.

I don't think she liked that my dad spent so much time with me and my mom. Once they got together, I started spending more time at his place in the city instead of him spending time at ours. Even after moving to Seattle, he kept an apartment in NYC for his weekends with me. Marnie preferred it that way.

I thought it was because she didn't like my mom. Maybe it was me she never liked.

"She said what?" Rhys says, his voice so quiet it's deadly.

"She said he coddled me," I repeat. "So she canceled my credit cards. She, um, she thinks I need to figure out how to be an adult and stop depending on his money." My cheeks heat with embarrassment. The last thing I want is for this man to think I'm a spoiled little rich girl. "I have no problem with finding a job and making my own way. But I have an internship and classes, and I volunteer. Had. I won't be graduating now."

"What the fuck?"

"She canceled my tuition for next year."

"The hell she did," he growls, plucking me up from his lap and depositing me on the sofa beside him. He rises to his feet like a pissed-off lion, all grace and deadly intent, his face carved from granite. "She has no say in your education, songbird."

"She does when my dad left her everything," I whisper.

He blinks at me, opens his mouth, and then blinks again. "Who told you that?"

"I guess I just assumed he left it to her."

"Brant didn't discuss his will with you?"

"He left me a majority stake in the company, but Marnie inherited everything else."

Rhys mutters a curse. "He didn't leave her everything, songbird," he says, shaking his head. "In fact, the only thing he left her was the house and his insurance policy. By rights, everything else is legally yours. He appointed her as the trustee of the estate, that's it. That means she oversees things on your behalf until you graduate from college, then it's yours to do with as you see fit."

"I..." This time, I blink, caught off-guard. Aside from the company, my dad and I never discussed any of this. No one ever discussed it with me. Not before the funeral. Not after the funeral. Not ever. I just assumed he left everything else to Marnie since they were married. Maybe I should have asked questions, though. But the last thing on my mind was his money. All I cared about was the fact that someone killed my dad.

"I'll take care of it," Rhys says grimly. "You will be graduating next year, and she won't be cutting you off from what's legally yours."

"I...thank you." I fidget uncomfortably. "Do you think...um...."

"What?"

"Can I stay with you?" I blurt before I lose the nerve. "I mean for a little while? I promise I won't get in your way. I just... I have nowhere else to go until classes resume, and she made it clear she doesn't want me there. I'll get a job. I'll clean or cook. I'll stay out of your way. I promise I won't be any trouble. But I'm not ready to go back to Boston yet. I have something to do here first."

"What do you have to do?" he asks, his expression sharp, hawkish...almost as intense as the question. And wow. If that's how he looks at suspects, he's probably good at his job. I'm not even a criminal, and I'm ready to confess.

"I need to find out who killed my dad," I say, squaring my shoulders.

"You need to find out who killed your dad," he repeats.

"Yes." I lift my chin in a show of bravery. Inside, my stomach quivers, and my heart beats a million miles a minute. I feel like I'm facing down Goliath. Only Goliath is a cop with a badge and the authority to arrest me. Or, at the very least, the power to turn me into the authorities who can arrest me.

"Why?" he asks, tilting his head to the side like I'm a mystery he's dying to solve.

"Because when I was five, I was terrified of the monsters under my bed," I say. "I thought they wanted to hurt me. My dad would come over every night and sleep in my room just so I'd sleep. This went on for two months straight. He barely got any sleep at all, but he did it so I could sleep. Now, I've learned there are actual monsters out there, only they weren't after me. They were after him. They killed him. And he won't rest easy until someone finds them. So until they're behind bars where they belong, I won't sleep either."

"Jesus," Rhys whispers, his eyes turning dark.

"It's been three months. Seattle has no leads, no suspects, nothing. It's like they aren't even looking." I push my hair back from my face, and the blanket slips. Rhys's gaze immediately falls to my chest. I'm still naked, my clothes forgotten on the bathroom floor. We never put the others on me. I swallow hard as he stares at me, his gaze locked on my exposed breast.

Is it my imagination, or did he just groan?

My nipple hardens, my flesh pebbling at the hungry, absorbed look on his face. No one has ever looked at me like he is right now. I squeeze my legs together, aching for things I know not to even consider. And yet I do consider them. In the dark of night, when the lights are off, I consider them all too often. How this man would feel above me. How he would taste. If his hands would glide roughly across my skin or if he'd be gentle. I think about him and touch myself. I moan his name and come apart in the dark, my own little secret. My own hidden shame.

I want him with an intensity that frightens me. It surpasses everything—music, a future on stage, the ache to have a big family. I'd give it all up for even a taste of this man. Some strong, independent woman I am, right? Willing to set aside everything I've ever dreamed about for even a moment with the one man I shouldn't want.

If my dad were here, he would never forgive me. He'd never forgive Rhys.

And yet I want him anyway.

"Cover up, songbird."

"Why?" I ask, suddenly defiantly angry. At him for not feeling the same way. At the universe for putting him in my path and placing him just out of reach. At Marnie for leaving me no choice but to come here. At…everything. "Does my body offend you?"

"Just cover up, Raven." He turns to face the opposite direction.

"Fine." I roll my eyes and yank the blanket up over my shoulder, clutching it to my chest like a wrap. "You can look now. All my rolls and parts are carefully tucked away so they don't blind you." I gather the clothes he collected for me in my free hand and climb to my feet, my throat burning with unshed tears. I'm acting like a brat, and that's not me.

I don't like it much. But a thousand different emotions all clamor for attention at once, throwing me off balance. I feel rejected and confused. I'm exhausted and sad. I desperately miss my dad. My stepmom kicked me out and cut me off. She lied to me. And I'm here, asking for help from the one man I should be staying far, far away from.

No, I'm not acting like myself. Right now, I'm not even sure who I am anymore.

I quietly slip past him to get dressed. At least that's my plan. Before I even make it two steps, he grabs me from behind. His arms are like vises around me, inexorably dragging me back into the broad wall of his chest. Even though I know I can't break his hold, I struggle anyway.

"You've been through hell today, so I'm going to let your little attitude slide," he rasps in my ear, his voice gritty. "But we're going to get one thing straight right now, princess. The only thing about your body that offends me is the fact that I don't know what every gorgeous inch of it tastes like."

I gasp, going limp in his arms as shock drains the fight right out of me.

"You're ravishing, and you know it. But you're Brant's daughter, and I'm trying real hard to be a gentleman here and pretend my cock hasn't been hard for you since you were eighteen," he says. "So I need you to keep that beautiful body covered while you're here, or your daddy's ghost is going to rip my balls out through my throat."

"Rhys, what–?"

His lips brush my temple, cutting me off before I can even figure out what I'm trying to ask him. What in the world is happening? What is he saying? What dream is this? I don't know, and I don't get the chance to figure it out.

"Go put on some clothes and then come back out here, song-bird," he says, gently setting me away from him. "We need to talk."

I stumble from the room on weak legs.

What the heck just happened?

Chapter Three

RHYS

"GODDAMN," I GROWL, JERKING my cock hard and fast. Visions of Raven play behind my eyelids. She's sprawled across my bed, her thick thighs spread wide, her lower lips glistening with her juices, the fingers of one hand buried in her cunt. The other pinches one cherry nipple. Her soft moans and the sound of her fingers thrusting into her wet cunt fill the room. So does her heady scent.

"Rhys," she moans. "Please, I need you."

I grip my shaft tight, twisting my wrist when I reach the head.

"Please. Fuck me." Those pretty blue eyes beg as sweetly as her lips. "I need to be yours."

My balls draw up, cum shooting up my shaft as I lose the fight. My stomach clenches, the bundle of nerves at the base of my spine tingling. I spill into my hand, biting my lip to stifle my groan.

I'm an asshole for jerking off to thoughts of her while she's getting dressed in the other room. There's no doubt about that. But it had to happen. Maybe it'll help me keep my damn hands off her while she's here.

A flash of her ivory skin floats to the surface of my mind, her hard nipple begging for my mouth around it.

"Maybe not," I mutter, reaching for the toilet paper to clean myself up. For a moment, I just stand there with a wad of it in my messy hand, pondering how utterly fucked I am. I'm in love with my dead best friend's daughter. She'll be living in my house all summer. She'll be mine to care for, mine to protect, mine to love. And by some miracle, I'm supposed to keep my hands to myself.

I'm not supposed to touch her. I'm not supposed to fuck my kid into her. I'm not supposed to fall harder. I'm supposed to be a consummate gentleman.

That's what Brant would expect. That's what any father would expect.

It's what she deserves. Especially now. Especially from me. She's here to find out who killed her father, for Christ's sake. She can't sleep because that question eats her alive. And I'm the asshole who could answer it for her. I could tell her exactly what she wants to know...and destroy her entire life in the process.

There will be no trust fund then. No company. No graduating from Berklee next year. No financially secure future. I have a feeling she'd give it all up without hesitation to know what I know. But the rest of it?

Would she want to know if it meant destroying her father's reputation? His company? Watching his name be dragged through the mud? Putting a target on the back of a baby? That's the part that fucks me up. If it were just his money at risk, I'd shout the truth from the fucking rooftops and not regret a second of it. But this is different.

Too much is at stake. One wrong move, and everything crumbles. I'm trying like hell to protect her here. To protect Brant and his memory. To protect his and Marnie's kid.

You're trying to protect yourself, you asshole.

Yeah, I guess that's true too. I'm a fucking coward for it, but I don't want to face a day when Raven looks at me and sees the monster I see when I look in the mirror. If she knew the truth, that's exactly what she'd see...not a man trying to protect her, but one who helped cover up her father's murder.

"Fuck," I growl, quickly cleaning up. I tuck my cock back in my pants and zip up before heading out of the guest bathroom. Raven's still in my bedroom, the door firmly shut. I breathe a sigh and head to the kitchen to clean up the case file from the old farm table before she sees it. There are some things she never needs to know, never needs to see. The shit in that file...well, she may want to know who killed Brant, but I guarantee she doesn't want to see those photos. She doesn't want to live with those memories.

I know because I do. Raven isn't the only one losing sleep. She isn't the only one chasing monsters. Except I made my bed. I get to lie in it.

Fuck you very much, Marnie.

In my life, I've only ever considered one woman a stone-cold bitch. My mother. Every other woman on this planet, I've found worthy of the utmost respect. They pull off miracles every day while we're standing around with our dicks in our hands, trying to figure out how the fuck they do it. They're brilliant, terrifying creations that should be protected at all costs. My mother, on the other hand, is a heartless, selfish, ruthless bitch.

I'm beginning to think Marnie Calloway is right up there with her. I actually felt sorry for her at first. She found out she was pregnant and found out her husband was playing mobster on the same day.

"Our baby. Oh my god, our baby!"

"You're pregnant?"

"I just got home from the doctor when I heard him in his office," she says through sobs, her arms wrapped around her body. "I wasn't trying to eavesdrop. I was just waiting until he was finished so I could share the news. But then I heard him..." She sobs bitterly. "He's been laundering dirty money through the company for years."

"Jesus Christ." I pace away from the couch. "You're sure?"

"He admitted it. He admitted e-everything." She sobs again. "I don't know what to do! If anyone finds out, they'll destroy him, Rhys. Jack will take everything."

She's not wrong. Jack Hale, his business partner, will dismantle Brant's empire brick by brick and the courts won't lift a finger to stop him. Hell, they'll help him do it. Brant will lose everything down to his freedom. Raven and the baby will be left with nothing. So will Marnie. Her fortune is tied up in Brant's company too.

Jesus Christ.

What the fuck are you into, Brant?

"What am I going to do, Rhys?" she whispers.

"Don't say anything to anyone about what you heard," I say, making a split-second decision. "Just go home and wait for me to figure this shit out."

I should never have sent her back there. I should have gone myself, confronted Brant, and demanded answers. If I had, maybe he'd still be alive. Instead, Marnie went home. Twenty-four hours later, Brant was dead. And she officially had me by the balls.

"What the fuck did you do, Marnie?" I yell, staring in shock at Brant's body on the security camera. Brant's body. Fucking Christ. He's dead. That's his blood spread across the floor. His blood splattered across the wall.

I spin away from the camera, my stomach heaving.

Fifteen years in law enforcement, and I've never puked on my shoes. Never shoved anything up my nose to mask the smell or shied away from the sights either. Figured if the victims could live those horrors, I owed them the respect of looking without throwing up on my goddamn shoes. I want to throw up now.

"I was just trying to get away from him!" Marnie cries. "He was yelling and acting crazy. I thought he was going to hurt me or the baby. I didn't mean to hurt him." Tears pour down her face,

her mascara running in rivulets down her cheeks. "I didn't know we were so close to the table or the fireplace. Now, what are we going to do, Rhys?"

"We? This is on you, Marnie."

"No, it's on us! I came to you for help. You're a cop, and you sent me back there! How do you think the world is going to feel when they hear that?" She dashes tears from her face, her expression twisting into something cold...ugly. She's not the same vain, self-absorbed woman I've known for the last four years. She's someone else. Someone desperate, on the edge. Someone dangerous. "How do you think Raven will feel when she finds out that you're partially responsible for this?"

"What the fuck are you talking about?"

"I'll tell everyone," she says, her shrill voice inching toward hysterical. "I'll tell the world that you sent me back there. I'll tell the world who he really was. I'll tell them everything. Will he still be a hero to his precious little Raven then, Rhys? Will you?"

When she came to me, did she already plan to kill him, or was it an accident like she said? I don't know. I wish to hell I did. His blood might not be on my hands, but everything that happened after, well, that certainly is. Marnie's still walking free because of me. If she goes down, we all do.

Tick, tick, boom, motherfucker.

I don't give a shit if I go. They can lock me up and throw away the key. At this point, it's less than I deserve. Marnie figured out long ago what Brant never realized. She saw the way I looked at Raven the day we met. She knew why I've avoided her for so long. She thought using that knowledge against me would muzzle me.

She's wrong.

Holding Raven's future over my head may have bought her a little time, but I'm not tame. I've let her run the show and pull the strings because she's pregnant and I won't let her go to prison while she's carrying Brant's kid. But she fucked up the minute she lashed out at Raven. When it comes to protecting what belongs to me, I bite. While I may not be able to take Raven to my bed, that doesn't make her any less mine.

I'll be on the first plane leaving the island as soon as the last raindrop falls. Marnie will be having a change of heart about cutting her off. My songbird will be finishing school on time. If Marnie intends to hold onto Brant's fortune by keeping Raven from graduating, that won't be happening. She'll play by my rules where Raven is concerned, or the only place we're going after Brant's kid is born is to prison. I'll destroy my own future to fuck her over without hesitation.

I just need time to sort out the details first and figure out what I'm missing. Whatever it is…I'm pretty fucking certain it's the key to this whole mess. It's the answer to why Brant was laundering money through his company. It's the answer to why Marnie killed him. Hell, maybe it's even the answer to why she dragged me into it and why she's trying to cut Raven out now.

There's always an inciting incident, something that starts the boulder rolling downhill. Trying to find it when you're missing half the puzzle is a pain in the ass.

"Um, hey," Raven says from the doorway behind me. "What's that?"

"Case file," I say, shoving the last few pages into the folder and then closing it.

"Oh. A big one?"

"Something like that." I tuck it under my arm, turning slowly to face her.

She looks like a little kid playing dress-up in my clothes, but damn, they look good on her. She tied the t-shirt up at her waist in a knot, allowing the tiniest sliver of her abdomen to show in brief, enticing flashes that already have my core temperature rising fifteen degrees. One sleeve hangs off her shoulder. Even dressed, she's far too tempting. Far too beautiful. She probably has to beat college boys off with a fucking stick.

Jealousy eats me alive at the thought. The little bastards don't even know what to do with a woman like her. They don't know how to eke out every drop of pleasure from that body, or how to take care of her after. They probably just pump until they cum and then pass out on top of her, not even caring if they got her off or if she enjoyed it. The bastards.

"Why are you growling at me?" she asks, her nose scrunching. "I'm completely covered."

Because I want to kill anyone who ever touched you.

Because I'd kill to be the only one who touches you ever again.

"Are you hungry?" I ask instead of opening that can of worms.

"Not really."

"Raven."

"I'm not hungry, Rhys."

"Bullshit. I can practically hear your stomach growling from here."

"Fine. Maybe I'm a little hungry," she says, averting her gaze. A pretty blush climbs up her cheeks, staining them pink. "I haven't eaten today."

I stare at her for a minute, perplexed as to why she didn't want to tell me that. And then realization dawns. I grit out a curse, my stomach sinking into my soles. "You're afraid of me."

She's a beautiful little songbird, all shy and sweet. Compared to her, I'm a gruff, mean bastard. Her world is probably full of pretty boys and rich assholes in designer duds. They learned to charm before they learned to talk. That's not me. I've spent too goddamn long working with criminals, visiting the places no one wants to go, dealing with the kinds of people no one wants to deal with. When you spend your life in the dark, the shadows stain you. They claimed me a long time ago.

Her wide, startled eyes meet mine. "What? No, I'm not."

"Then why'd you lie to me?"

"You don't like me much," she whispers. "I don't want to be a bother."

I stare at her for a full five count, caught off-guard. And then I shake my head and cross to the fridge. "Sit down, princess. I'll make you something to eat." I set the folder on top of the fridge and start pulling out stuff to make her a sandwich. "Why do you think I don't like you?"

"You were mean to me the first time we met." She shuffles across the kitchen to the table. Halfway there, a clap of thunder rattles the windowpanes, and she squeaks like a little mouse and then laughs self-consciously. "Sorry."

"Never apologize for being you," I say, watching as she pulls out a chair and sinks gracefully into it. She moves like a dream. I bet she danced when she was younger. Her body flows from one movement to the next like a ballerina's. Shit, I wish more ballerinas looked like her. I might actually watch the shit instead of sleeping through it when my stepmom forces me to go every Christmas. There's something beautiful about watching a curvy woman move. It's erotic as hell. "Make all the noise you want. This place could use it."

"You don't like the quiet?"

"Depends on the day."

"It's never quiet in Boston," she says almost wistfully. "New York City either. I might make too much noise just to fill the silence. I've never had much peace and quiet before. I may not like it much. Hopefully, I'll be able to find a job soon and won't have to stay here long."

"Uh, fuck no," I growl, dropping all the sandwich stuff onto the slate gray island.

She blinks wide eyes at me.

"You aren't working."

"I need a job, Rhys. I can't live off my savings forever."

"You won't need to live off your savings," I say, reaching for the loaf of bread. "Marnie and I will be having a discussion as soon as I can get to Seattle. She can't cut you off from what rightfully belongs to you."

"I don't want to cause any trouble."

"You aren't."

She falls silent, staring out the windows. With dark falling, there isn't much to see. The water is inky black, Orcas Island invisible behind the wall of rain still falling. Not that she's really trying to see any of that anyway. The kitchen reflects back in the glass. She's watching me and trying to be sneaky about it. It's cute that she thinks I don't know what she's doing.

I don't call her on it, though.

"I'm sorry I was a dick to you," I say instead.

She turns back to me.

"The day we met," I clarify. "It wasn't because I disliked you."

"Oh."

"Can we start over?"

"I've cried all over you more than I'd like to admit. And you've seen me naked. I think it's too late to start over, Rhys." She laughs softly, the subdued sound both rich and burbling. Her voice has power. Then again, I already knew that. She sells out every performance she books. "But maybe we can pretend we met for the first time when you picked me up at the airport for my dad's funeral?"

"Hell no," I growl. "I'm not pretending I didn't see you in that swimsuit, songbird."

"You remember that?" A pretty blush creeps across her cheeks.

"You think I'd forget you looking like a goddess?" I scoff at the thought, slathering mayo on a piece of bread. "I couldn't keep my eyes off you, Raven. That's why I was a dick."

"Oh," she whispers. "I thought you were annoyed I was there. Marnie was." A tiny frown pulls her lips down at the corners, crinkling her brows. "She didn't want her friends to see me in that swimsuit. She thought it was inappropriate."

"Marnie's a shallow, self-absorbed bitch."

Raven's eyes go wide.

"It's true." I shrug unapologetically. "She likes to be the center of attention. If anything draws attention from her, she can't stand it. It's part of why she loved your dad so much. He was always happy to show her off and let her have the spotlight as often as she wanted it." I scrape the butter knife on the side of the mayo jar and set it aside before piling turkey on the bread. "If she didn't like you in that swimsuit, it wasn't because she thought it was inappropriate. It was because she couldn't stand the thought of you outshining her."

"No one outshines Marnie. She's beautiful."

"You're right," I say with a wry snort. "She is beautiful. But that's all she is. She's something pretty to look at it. She's not interesting. She's not talented. She's not driven, compassionate, kind, loving, affectionate, warm, or funny. There are a million things she could be, but she chose to be none of them. The only thing she has to offer the world is beautiful." I rake my eyes down Raven's body, my gaze pointed. "You're the whole package—beauty, brains, talent, and heart. You outshine her, princess. She knows it. I know it. Everyone at that party knew it. You need a mirror if you don't see it too."

Raven dips her head, shyly looking at the tabletop.

Jesus. I love how sweet she is. It confuses the hell out of me at the same time. How does she not already know how incredible she is? Whoever she's been dating has done a piss-poor job taking care of her. She shouldn't have a single doubt in her mind about how beautiful she is.

"She's in for a rude awakening when she has this baby," I say, trying not to think too hard about the assholes who have put their hands on her.

"Baby?" she squeaks. "Marnie's *pregnant?*"

"Fuck." I lift my gaze to hers again, reading the shock written across her face. "You didn't know."

She shakes her head, her expression completely dumbstruck. *Son of a bitch.*

"I thought she told you."

Why the fuck didn't Marnie tell her? What game is she playing here?

"No," Raven whispers, her face pale. She swallows hard, unable to hide the hurt in her eyes. "She didn't tell me. Um, how...how far along is she?"

"A little over four months. They found out two days before..." I trail off awkwardly, ready to strangle Marnie. "Brant never got a chance to tell you. I assumed Marnie would tell you after the funeral."

"She never told me." A powerful sadness passes through her expression, making her look younger, lost in a way she hasn't since Brant died. She quickly blinks it away, putting on a brave face. "She never liked me much. I guess this just confirms that I'm not family in her opinion. But I'm...happy for her. I'm happy for my dad. I wish he were here."

"Me too," I say simply. "He'd be fucking thrilled about this kid."

"Right?" She smiles a tremulous, watery smile. "He always loved kids. I bet he was so excited when he found out. I'm glad he knew before he..." She trails off with a sigh. "I mean, I'm glad the last news he got was good news, you know? He deserved that."

I'm sorry, princess. Christ, I'm so fucking sorry.

"Yeah, he did," I agree.

We lapse into silence for a moment, both lost in our own thoughts. She watches me in the windows. I watch her from the corner of my eye. Neither of us speaks as I finish putting her sandwich together. We just watch one another, both pretending we aren't. Both pretending the silence between us isn't charged. Both pretending we can handle this thing between us like adults out of respect for Brant's memory. I think we both know we're lying to ourselves.

It's only a matter of time before one of us cracks and crumbles.

We aren't two ships passing in the night. We're the RMS Emerald and the SS Storstad on a collision course in the fog.

We're the Titanic headed for certain disaster as we drift off course.

One way or another, she'll escape unscathed. Even if I have to bleed to make it happen.

"What did you want to talk about?" she asks suddenly.

"You."

"Me?" Another tiny frown. "What about me?"

"About you staying here."

"Oh."

"I have rules."

"Keep myself covered," she says, rolling her eyes.

"No," I growl, dumping chips onto her plate before starting on my own sandwich. "That's not a rule, Raven. That's me trying to do the right thing. Brant would have ripped my balls off if he knew the things I've thought about doing to you."

She watches me silently for a moment, thinking about something. I know the moment she gathers the nerve to say it. I see it in her eyes. I watch determination cross her face and lift her chin. I see it subtly change the air around her. She changes from shy little lamb to confident woman, exactly like she does when she steps onto the stage.

"I've thought about things too, Rhys," she says, her voice soft. "More than I should. For longer than I should have."

"Jesus." I narrowly avoid slicing my finger open instead of the tomato.

"The first time I saw you, I was attracted to you. But you were his best friend. I know that makes you untouchable. I know that makes the things I want wrong." She glances away. "It doesn't make me want them any less."

"There is nothing wrong with you," I rasp, heat in my voice. "Don't ever think otherwise."

"If you say so," she says doubtfully.

My stomach churns, my guts twisting at the realization that she thinks she's bad for wanting me. It's one thing for me to feel that way, but for her to feel it? Unacceptable. There is nothing bad or wrong or less than perfect about her. Not a damn thing.

"What are your rules?" she asks before I can tell her that.

I hesitate, unsure if I should drag us back to the other conversation. And then I reluctantly decide to let it go for now. Nothing good will come of talking about the way we both feel. It won't change anything. She's still Brant's kid. I'm still unworthy of her. That won't change. It can't, not when she doesn't know the truth.

"Rule number one, you're here for summer vacation," I say. "That means you spend your summer enjoying yourself as much as possible. You aren't my maid. You aren't responsible for me. You don't have to earn your keep to stay here. You stay for as long as you want, and you spend the time doing what you want."

"What if I want to cook or clean?"

"One day a week."

"Three."

"Two, final offer."

"Agreed."

"Rule number two, you don't go out on the rocks or on the water alone. The island is beautiful, but it's dangerous. Don't underestimate it," I order. "Too many people get cocky and get in over their heads. If you get yourself hurt, I'm going to be pissed."

"I think I can agree to that," she says.

"Rule number three, no investigating your dad's death."

"No way."

"Raven, you don't even know what you're looking at or what you're looking for," I say. "You don't know the first thing about criminal investigations. The best you can hope for is that you don't fuck up Seattle's case or end up in a jail cell or a victim yourself."

"I have a right to ask questions." She shoots me a mulish, mutinous look.

"And what happens if you ask the right questions to the wrong people?" I press. "What happens if you end up with the wrong attention on you? What do you do then?"

"I..." She trails off, her eyes narrowing as they crawl slowly across my face, carefully scrutinizing my expression. "You know something, don't you?"

I grit my teeth, refusing to answer.

"You do!" she cries. "You know something about what happened to him, don't you?"

"Raven."

"Are you looking into it? Do you have a suspect?" she asks. "Do you think they might come after me? Is that why you don't want me looking into it?"

"I didn't say that."

"Then why don't you want me looking into it?"

"Because there are some things you can't unknow, princess," I say, dropping the top piece of bread onto my sandwich. I carry our plates across the kitchen, setting her plate in front of her. "There are some things that stay with you forever. When you look into a crime, the first thing you dig into is the victim. You cut into the heart of him and reveal all his secrets...the good, the bad, and the ugly. What you find alters your perception of the victim forever."

"You think he had secrets."

"Everyone has secrets, songbird."

She swallows audibly, her expression troubled. She knows I'm right. Look at the two of us. We've been carrying our own secrets for the last three years, haven't we? Desperately trying to hide them from the very man we now mourn.

"You know his secrets, don't you?" she asks, watching my face intently.

I nod once, not lying to her.

"Are they...bad?"

"They aren't good," I admit.

Her face falls.

"Did...did they get him killed?"

"I can't answer that."

"Can't or won't?"

"I'm not sure yet," I say. It's the truth. I know enough to answer some of her questions, but not enough to answer all of them. Did Marnie kill him because of his secrets? Was it an accident like she claimed? Or did she have some other plan I haven't yet unraveled? I want to believe it was an accident, but nothing makes sense. Why did she drag me into it? Why blackmail me into helping her cover it up? I'm missing something and I don't know what.

"You don't want to tell me."

"He's your father, songbird. I'm trying to protect you."

"From what?" she asks, desperation in her voice. "I don't understand, Rhys."

"I know you don't," I sigh, tucking a strand of hair behind her ear. It's silky soft. "I need you to trust me, Raven. I know I'm asking for a lot right now, but trust that everything I've done and everything I'm doing is to protect you, your baby brother or sister, and Brant. I'll do whatever I have to do to ensure you're safe and taken care of. And I'll do everything I can to ensure that whoever killed Brant pays for it."

"Promise me," she demands. "Promise you'll make them pay for it."

"I swear to you, even if I have to destroy myself to do it, there will be justice," I vow, meaning every word. One way or another, Marnie will suffer the consequences for everything she's done. I don't care what it takes. As soon as she has that baby and I find a way to ensure Raven doesn't lose everything, she's done.

Raven scrutinizes my expression, searching out any little hint that I'm just telling her what she wants to hear to get her to give me what I want. When she doesn't find it, she expels a slow breath. "Okay," she reluctantly agrees. "I'll let you handle it."

Chapter Four

RAVEN

"Excuse me," I say, leaning over the bar to get the attention of the middle-aged bartender.

"Be right with you, hon," she says, not even glancing up from the long line of shot glasses set up in front of her. She grabs a bottle of tequila from beneath the bar and flips it upside down, quickly filling the glasses one by one. Somehow, she manages to do it without even spilling a drop.

It's impressive. I would have poured it all over everything had I tried that. Then again, serving alcohol isn't something I've ever done before. I've never drank much of it either. My schedule has always been so jam-packed that it never left a lot of room for going out or partying.

My whole life, I've wanted to sing. I've poured everything into it. And I'm *good* at it. Really good. Unfortunately, I'm not great at much else. I never had time to master anything outside of music. It's worrisome. If Rhys can't convince Marnie to let me finish school, I'm screwed. I'll be a mostly trained vocalist with no real-world skills beyond teaching kids to sing.

The bartender places the shot glasses on a tray with a bowl of lemon wedges and lifts a hand, waving over a waitress. As soon as she's sure the waitress is headed in her direction, she turns to me. Her brown eyes rake over me in a cursory assessment. If she recognizes me from any of the thousand news stories about my dad, she doesn't react. Her heavily made-up face gives nothing away.

"If you're drinking, I'm going to need to see some ID," she says.

"Oh, no." I quickly shake my head. "I'm not drinking. The guy at the door told me I should talk to you. Um, I found this on a bulletin board?" I thrust the flyer over the bar toward her. "Are you still looking for musicians?"

She takes the flyer and glances it over. Her eyes come back to me for another assessment. This one lasts half a beat longer than the first. "You're a musician?"

"Yes. I sing and play piano and guitar."

"What genre?"

"I'm trained in contemporary music, but I can sing anything from opera to the blues to R&B."

She eyes me for a long, silent moment. "Sing something for me."

"Right here?" My gaze darts around the bar. It's only a little after three in the afternoon, but the place is packed. I think the whole island rushed outside as soon as it stopped storming this morning. When I made it downtown a few hours ago, cars were pouring off the ferries in an endless parade. This little island is overwhelmingly busy.

It's not hard to see why. The entire island is breathtaking. The coast offers a thousand different, beautiful views. Inland, the coast gives way to farmland and dozens of interesting farmstands to explore. Downtown Friday Harbor has everything from restaurants to bars to unique little shops. I've been exploring for hours, and I still haven't even made a dent in it.

I needed something to keep me occupied, though. As soon as the storm cleared, Rhys left for Seattle. He wanted me to go with him, but I didn't think that was the best idea. Marnie already hates me. I'd rather not make it worse, especially since she's carrying my little brother or sister. If she doesn't let me see the baby, it'll break my heart.

I don't understand why she didn't tell me she's pregnant. What did I ever do to her to make her hate me so much? I know she loved my dad and she's hurting. I loved him too. But we should be helping each other through this, not pushing each other away. She shouldn't be alone right now.

When I lost my mom, the only thing that got me through it was not being alone. My dad came to Boston and stayed for weeks after the funeral. He dropped everything to be there for me just to make sure I was okay. He took care of packing up Mom's apartment in New York, dealing with the insurance, everything. I needed him so much.

Marnie needs people right now too. She's pregnant and she just lost her husband. I feel bad for being so upset with her yesterday. Of course she doesn't want me lounging around the house all summer. She doesn't want to have to take care of me too. Why should she? She has enough to deal with right now. We should be taking care of her, not the other way around.

"Right here," the bartender confirms.

I inhale a breath and push thoughts of Marnie and my dad from my mind, trying to focus on the here and now. Marnie wants me to take responsibility for myself. Here's my chance. I just need to convince this woman to give me a shot.

My hands shake, my nerves fluttering as the noise coming from the bar intrudes. It's loud. Crowded. Hot.

Don't think about it, I coach myself. *This is no different than singing on stage. You can do this. Easy.*

"Do you have any requests?" I ask.

"Whatever you want," she says, eyeing me like she expects me to vomit all over her bar at any moment. And that look...the doubt in her eyes...somehow that steadies my nerves.

I'm used to people doubting me. They've been doing it my whole life. As soon as they find out who my father is, they assume I'm just another spoiled little rich girl coasting through on daddy's money instead of her own talent. They think because I'm a big girl, I don't belong. Or because I'm quiet, I don't fit. They take one look at me and assume they know what I'm capable of.

They're wrong. I've been proving them wrong every single day since I was thirteen.

The only song that comes to mind is *Islands in the Stream* by Dolly Parton and Kenny Rogers, so I take a breath, count it off...and belt it out. The bartender's eyes widen as if she's surprised. I'm not sure how much she wants to hear, but she doesn't stop me, so I keep singing.

The bar falls quiet, but I barely notice. When I'm singing, the rest of the world disappears for a little while. The only things that exist are the rise and fall of my voice and the song. I get lost in the lyrics. Between those notes, for just a little while, I'm not alone in the world. I'm riding on the backs of giants, untouched by the painful truths that wait when the music dies. My world isn't crumbling around me. My parents aren't gone. I'm not hopelessly in love with a man I can't have. Everything is exactly the way it should be.

"Well, hot damn," the bartender says when the last note fades. "You can *sing*."

Everyone in the bar claps and whistles.

"Thank you," I whisper, blushing.

"What's your name, hon?"

"Raven. Um, Raven Calloway."

"Raven, I'm Tawnie McAllister. I own the place." She extends one hand over the bar for me to shake.

I take it, giving it a firm shake like my father taught me. "It's nice to meet you, Tawnie," I say. "Your bar is lovely."

She snorts. "This place passed lovely thirty years ago, honey. There's more beer and sweat in these floorboards than hardwood. But the bar is mine and the tourists love it, so I'm not complaining. You sing professionally, Raven?"

"I'm a voice student at Berklee in Boston."

She nods. "Are you going to be on the island long?"

"I'll be here for the summer at least. I'm not sure about after that," I say carefully.

"We have a talent test coming up on Friday night," she says. "You perform and we pass the bucket. The acts that pull in the most in tips get added to the schedule. You interested?"

"Yes! Definitely."

She grins at me. "You sing like you just did, and I don't think you'll have a problem securing your spot in the rotation. For weekdays, we pay a flat fee, plus you keep your tips. On weekends, you keep whatever we make at the door, your flat fee, plus tips. During the season, we see a lot of traffic through here. With a voice like yours, it can mean good money. Not great money, but good."

"It sounds perfect," I say, trying to remain professional even though I want to jump up and down and squeal with excitement. The money won't come anywhere close to what I need to pay my tuition, but it'll be mine. It won't be something given to me by my father or Marnie or anyone else. No one can take it away or say I didn't earn it. For once, I'll be making my own way.

The ground solidifies beneath my feet.

"One sec," Tawnie says, making her way to the opposite end of the bar. Her wide hips roll with every step in her painted-on jeans. She has to be in her sixties, but she isn't dressed like it. She reminds me of one of the women from an old 80s movie. Big hair, heavy makeup, bright clothes. She's as unique as this island. I like her.

She grabs a clipboard off the wall before making her way back to me.

"I've got two spots left," she says, flipping through the papers clipped to the board. "One at nine and one at ten. Which do you want?"

"Which is busiest?"

"Smart girl," she says, grinning at me over the top of the board. "I'll put you down for nine. The last ferry for the night leaves at ten. People start clearing out around nine-thirty."

"That sounds perfect. Thank you so much, Tawnie."

"We'll see you Friday. You get one song, so make it count."

"I will," I promise, give her my contact information, then hurry out the door before she can change her mind. As soon as I step outside, the breeze blowing in from the water hits me, the scent of brine filling the air. The dull roar of the bar fades, replaced by the hum of traffic, and the purr of the boats on the water. There are so many of them, it's like a constant traffic jam out there, and yet there's order to the chaos. Everyone knows exactly where they're going and what they're doing.

I fish my phone out of my pocket to text Rhys.

Does a gig count as a job? Asking for a friend...

I don't think he'll be upset about it. Crap. Maybe I should have asked first?

"No way," I whisper to myself. If there's one thing my dad taught me, it was that it's better to ask for forgiveness than permission. I'm a big girl. This is my life, my choice. I appreciate Rhys for wanting to look out for me, but I *need* to do this. Not for Marnie or for him, but for me. To prove to myself that I can. If I manage to graduate, I'll be responsible for a multi-billion-dollar company. How can I do that when I can't even take care of myself?

I've wallowed and cried and let myself drown in self-pity and grief for three months. Now, it's time to put on my big girl panties and find out who I am. I may be an orphan, but I refuse to let that be my defining trait. I'm not going to be the hapless girl who allows life to happen to her. I'm not going to curl up quietly and just give up.

And I'm not giving up on finding out who killed my dad either. I'm going to prove to Rhys that I'm strong enough to handle whatever he thinks he's protecting me from.

I spent most of the night wracking my brain, trying to come up with an answer, but nothing fit. My dad was honestly the most boring billionaire on the planet. What does Rhys know that's so bad he thinks it'll change the way I see my dad?

"Stop thinking," I mutter to myself. "You aren't allowed to think anymore."

Two teen girls walking past look at me oddly and then fall into a fit of laughter when they pass me. They quickly shush each other, only to laugh again.

I tip my head forward and groan. Guess I deserved that one, talking to myself on a busy sidewalk.

I'm blaming Rhys. He touched me yesterday and turned my brain to literal mush. Never in a million years did I expect him to say any of the things he said to me yesterday. He called me beautiful. He said he wants me, that he's always wanted me. That he thinks about doing things to me. It's odd, feeling like you're on top of the world and circling the drain at the exact same moment.

I've dreamed about him saying those things to me for years. But hearing them...well, hearing them didn't make me feel any better. It just reminded me that I can't have him. He's still untouchable. Only now it's worse. Because I know he wants to touch me too. That should make it better, but it doesn't.

I heave a sigh and start down the sidewalk, headed back toward his house. My buoyant mood is gone, my heart and mind heavy. What am I going to do? What are we going to do? Live together all summer and pretend there's nothing between us? Am I supposed to watch him date other women?

I won't survive that. The first time I see him with someone, it'll break me. I know it will.

My phone buzzes in my hand. I stop walking to read the message.

Rhys: Depends. Do I get to attend this gig?

Me: You want to hear me sing?
Rhys: Hell yes.
Me: Really?
Rhys: Yes. Am I invited?
Me: Yes, but I have conditions.
Rhys: Wait. Where is this gig?
Me: McAllister's on Friday.
Rhys: Yeah, no. I'm definitely fucking coming, princess.
Me: Wait. Why? Is it not reputable?

I wait anxiously for him to text me back, but he doesn't. Instead, my phone rings. I immediately swipe to answer. "Please tell me people don't get shot in the bar or something," I say. "Tawnie didn't mention anything nefarious."

"No one's been shot in a bar in Friday Harbor in years, songbird," he says. "Fights break out regularly, but that's every bar and restaurant in town. Drunk tourists are a pain in my ass."

"Oh." I exhale a relieved sigh. "That's good then. Well, not the drunk tourists fighting part. That has to be annoying."

"Very," he says drily.

"What's the problem with McAllister's?"

"The fact that there are too many men there," he growls.

"There are?" I frown, trying to remember the crowd inside. It didn't look like there were an overwhelming number of men to me. Just a normal amount. Maybe it's different on the weekends, though? "How many?"

"One is too many."

"Rhys."

My stomach flutters. Lord, this man knows exactly how to make my knees weak.

"They'll be drinking and watching you on stage, thinking about trying to claim you before someone else can," he growls, his voice somehow lethally soft and bristling with rage at the same time. "Fuck no, princess. New rule. You don't date. Men don't exist to you while you're here."

"Fine, then you don't date either," I throw right back at him.

"Never do," he says. "It drives me fucking crazy thinking about someone else touching you. I want to kill anyone who has ever put their goddamn hands on you, songbird."

"Then I guess it's a good thing no one ever has."

"What?"

The sudden intensity in his voice breaks through the fog he's putting me under. Crap. I just told him I'm a virgin. That wasn't supposed to slip out. I'm twenty-one and I've only ever been kissed once. I was sixteen. It lasted for all of five seconds, and we never spoke again.

"Say it again, Raven," he growls.

"I said I guess it's a good thing no one has ever touched me," I say.

"You're a virgin."

"Yes," I whisper, glancing around like I'm sharing state secrets or something.

"Name your conditions."

"What?"

"Your conditions. Name them," he says, his voice tight. Strained.

"Oh. Um, you can't tip me. And you have to watch me from backstage."

"Deal."

Well, that was easier than I thought it would be.

"Where are you?" he asks. His voice still sounds odd...intense.

"I'm walking back to your place."

"Good. I'll be there as soon as I can."

"Okay."

"See you soon, songbird."

"Bye, Rhys," I whisper.

Chapter Five

RHYS

"WHAT ARE YOU DOING here?" Marnie says, her blue eyes full of genuine surprise. Her blonde hair is piled up on her head, strands hanging freely around her heart-shaped face. Her small bump is obvious in her designer dress. She doesn't look like a grieving widow. She's fresh-faced, glowing. Brant would be over the moon to see her this way.

"We need to talk."

"Oh." Annoyance filters across her face. Raven was dead wrong about her last night. She doesn't outshine anyone. She's beautiful the same way scorpions are. They may be pretty to look at, but they're cold and uncaring. She put on a good act and fooled us all for a while, but the mask is off now. There is no unseeing the truth once it's out. "Can it wait? I'm in the middle of something right now."

"Nope." I step around her into the house, not giving her an opportunity to shut the door in my face or bar me from entering. We're having this conversation now. I don't give a fuck what she has going on. Whatever it is can wait.

I do a cursory sweep of the foyer and living room, trying not to look too hard at anything. Coming here is always a punch in the gut. I've spent countless hours on that couch, watching the Seahawks with Brant on the television hidden behind the panel, or playing poker at the antique table in the corner. Every part of the house is lavish and expensive. But it's a home too.

I frown when I see Jack Hale standing on the far side of the living room, a glass of brandy in his hand. He's staring out the French doors into the backyard.

"Rhys! Are you kidding me right now?" Marnie growls from behind me.

Jack turns when he hears her.

"Rhys," he says, giving me a head-to-toe sweep. Jack never liked me much. As far as he's concerned, I was always just the hired help, someone levels beneath him. He's old money. Cocky. Arrogant. A hell of a businessman.

"Jack," I say, giving him a chin-lift. "Sorry to interrupt, but I have an urgent matter to discuss with Marnie."

"No problem." He brushes back the sleeve of his jacket to glance at his watch. "We were finishing up anyway, and I've got another meeting." He tips back his glass, draining the amber liquid. "I'll have my assistant send the paperwork through for you to look over, Marnie."

"Do that," she says, her voice cool. I can feel her glaring daggers at my back.

He deposits his glass on the sideboard and then picks his briefcase up from the floor. Marnie stands stiffly when he kisses her on the cheek. She doesn't even look at him. She's too busy glaring at me.

What the fuck did Brant ever see in her?

Jack murmurs something to her, which prompts her to shake her head. He says something else, earning a grunt from her. This pisses him off. He tenses slightly. It's so subtle I don't think anyone else would have noticed, but I do. Reading people is what I do for a living.

And I'm reading a whole hell of a lot right now.

Marnie pulls away from Jack, who finally takes the hint. He's not thrilled about it, but he backs off and stalks toward the door, cold as ice.

"Nice seeing you, detective," he says on his way out the door. He doesn't mean it.

I don't return the platitude.

"What do you want, Rhys?" Marnie demands as soon as the door closes behind him.

"For you to do your fucking job as the executor of Raven's trust."

"Of course this is about Raven." She rolls her eyes. "God, you're just like him when it comes to her, you know that? She bats those lashes, and you fall all over yourself rushing to her aid. It's ridiculous."

"He was her father," I grit out.

"What's your excuse?"

"You cut her off," I say instead of engaging. I'm not surprised she's jealous of Raven. Raven is beautiful, talented, and smart, and people are genuinely drawn to her. She doesn't have to work to be liked. It's effortless for her. Marnie knows she can't compete. It drives her nuts that she wasn't the center of Brant's world. I think she thought once he moved to Seattle, he'd be all hers, and that didn't happen. He didn't stop being Raven's father. I think Marnie knows if she'd pushed, he would have chosen Raven over her, and she hates Raven for it. She loved Brant.

"Don't be so melodramatic, Rhys. I canceled her credit cards," Marnie says with a laugh. "She's almost twenty-two. She's more than capable of providing for herself when she isn't in school."

"You canceled her tuition payment for next year," I growl, still furious about that.

Marnie gasps. "I did not!"

"Raven certainly thinks you did."

"If that's what she told you, she's lying."

"And I suppose she's lying about you telling her that she isn't welcome here too?" I ask, crossing my arms and planting my feet. She's full of shit and we both know it.

"I was upset," she sniffs, averting her gaze. "I can't stand seeing her, Rhys. How am I supposed to live with her for three months? It's like looking at him." She shudders. "I can't do it. I don't need to be reminded of that time."

"You don't need to be reminded of that time? Jesus fucking Christ, Marnie." I laugh without mirth. "You killed her father, but you're the victim here? Do you even hear yourself?"

"Of course I do!" she cries, throwing her hands up in the air. "Of course, I know how it sounds." Tears swim in her eyes. "But I'm pregnant with his baby. That's hard enough without having to look into Raven's eyes every day and deal with that guilt too."

"At least you feel guilt," I mutter.

"You think I don't?" she asks.

I shrug, not sure I believe she does. Not sure I believe a fucking word she says. She's like one of those children's toys that you draw on and then wipe clean. She can be whoever she wants to be. When the show is over, she just erases the face and starts over. The only problem is that eventually, the magnetic ink begins to stick to the board. Little bits of the old drawings remain. They get all mixed up with the new. Sooner or later, the whole board is so messed up that you can't tell what you're looking at anymore.

"I feel it every day," she whispers. "Every day. He was the love of my life."

I'm no longer sure I believe that either. Did she love Brant? Yes. I still believe that much. But I don't know if she loved him when she killed him. I'm beginning to think she stopped loving him a long time ago. Her jealousy of Raven poisoned her. It destroyed Brant. I'll be damned before I let it destroy Raven too.

"I've kept my mouth shut and played your little game because you're carrying his kid," I say quietly. "But you're paying her tuition and you're sending her new cards. You're going to treat her with the respect she deserves and you're going to stop playing fucking games with her trust. If you don't, the only time you'll hold that kid is when you're giving birth in a prison ward."

"You wouldn't," she says.

"Try me."

"You'll go down too."

"I know." I hold her gaze, not blinking. "The difference between you and me, Marnie? You pretend to feel guilt. I actually feel it. I deserve to rot in a fucking prison for helping you. If taking you down means I go down with you, so be it."

For the first time, doubt enters her expression, followed by the first inklings of fear. She knows I mean it. Good. "You don't mean that," she whispers anyway. "It was an accident, Rhys."

"Pay her tuition, Marnie," I growl, stepping around her to the door. "Don't test me."

"Rhys, wait! I'll pay the tuition. Of course, I will. But you aren't doing her any favors with the credit cards," she says. "You may think I'm some monster, but I'm not. I'm trying to help her. She's never had the chance to figure out what she's made of because Brant was always there to rescue her. Now, she's on her own. She needs to prove to herself that she can take care of herself."

"No," I say softly, pulling the door open. "You're on your own, Marnie. Raven isn't. She'll never be on her own. She'll never be you."

"And when she graduates, she'll be in charge of Brant's company," she snaps. "How do you expect her to run a company when she doesn't even know what she's capable of doing? You think you're doing her some big favor by swooping in to save the day, but you aren't. All you're doing is ensuring that she fails before she ever has a chance to succeed."

"I know exactly what she's capable of," I say. "You're the one underestimating her and we both know you're doing it because you're desperate to hold onto his company. You can lie to yourself and pretend this is about you helping her if that makes you sleep better at night, but you can't lie to me. You aren't getting the company, Marnie. I'll burn the entire fucking thing to the ground before I let that happen."

Chapter Six

RAVEN

"Can I ask you a question?" I blurt, not even waiting for the front door to close behind Rhys

He rakes his sunglasses down his nose, pinning me with a look that makes my stomach quiver and jump. His half-smirk sends my heart into overdrive. How he's still single, I don't know. The man is ridiculously hot, especially when he's dressed for work. I never knew a man carrying a badge and a gun could be sexy, but this one is.

"You been working up the nerve to ask me this question long?" he asks.

"Only most of the day," I admit with a rueful laugh, tucking my legs under me on the sofa. As usual, he reads me like a book. He's scary good at it. It's been two days since he went to see Marnie. I don't know how he did it, but she paid my tuition. I got the email yesterday. She texted to tell me that she was sending new credit cards to me too. I told her not to worry about it. She never responded to that message. I know she read it though.

I've been dying to know what happened, but he hasn't shared. He hasn't said anything at all about it, in fact. When I told him I got the email, he just grunted and said good. I'm not sure what that means, but it's driving me crazy.

Rhys and I have settled into a…I don't know what to call it, honestly. Anytime I'm within five feet of him, my body aches. It feels like the air around me catches fire. I want to throw myself into his arms and let the flames consume us. I know he feels it too. But somehow, we've both managed to keep our hands to ourselves. Whenever I feel myself slipping, I blurt my dad's name.

He knows what I'm doing when I do it. He doesn't call me on it. Instead, he shares some memory of my dad, or I do. It's helped in more ways than one. Being able to talk about him with someone who loved him just as much as I do is healing. For once, I don't feel completely alone with my grief. I don't cry myself to sleep at night.

We remember and we laugh.

"What's your question, songbird?" He tosses his glasses on the table by the door. His badge goes next. He'll keep the gun on his hip until he gets to his room. That goes in the safe. I'm not sure if he's always so careful with it or if he's just extra cautious because I'm here.

"What happened with Marnie?"

"Your guess is as good as mine," he mutters. "Women like her poison themselves until they're bitter, miserable, and die alone. My mother is the same way."

"Really?" I frown, pulling a throw pillow into my lap. "I didn't know that."

"Don't talk about her much."

"I'm sorry."

He shrugs. "She didn't raise me. My stepmom did." A smile overtakes his face, lighting him up. "She's a real mom. She'd do anything for me. I have a little sister, Cassia. She isn't my dad's kid, but my stepmom would do anything for her too. As far as she's concerned, Cassia is family too."

"My mom was great too," I whisper, squeezing the pillow. "She was a singer like me. When I was younger, she'd take me with her sometimes while she busked in the subway. It was so much fun to watch her. People just loved her energy. Life with her was an adventure."

"I'm sorry you lost her."

"You sent me flowers." He sent the biggest bouquet of pink, white, and purple lilies and carnations. They were beautiful. The rest of the flowers went to nursing homes, but I kept his until every last petal died.

"I did," he says, his voice soft. His forest eyes are even softer. "I hate that I couldn't be there, princess." Sometimes, he looks at me like I'm the only thing he sees. Like he's just waiting for me to tell him that I'm his, and he'll betray every belief he's ever held to keep me. In those moments, the words climb up my throat like an aria, desperate to burst free. I want to utter them. I want to set us both free. So damn bad.

Does he know how much? Can he see me falling deeper?

"Rhys, I…"

"Jack Hale," he blurts.

I blink twice. "What?"

"Jack Hale was there when I got there," he says.

"Oh." I frown, trying to drag myself back from the ledge. Back to reality. I can't tell him that I'm in love with him. I can't set us free. He may want me, but that's not the same as what I feel. Besides, he's still keeping secrets. Big ones. "Why was Jack there?"

"Good question," he mutters, scrubbing a hand down his face. He looks weary, tired all the way to his bones. "They were allegedly meeting about something business related."

"You don't believe that." It's not a question. I've gotten pretty good at reading him too.

"I've been to business meetings with Jack," he says. "He never drinks when business is on the table. And Marnie never discusses business at home. Brant was banished to his home office for any and all business discussions."

"So maybe they weren't meeting about the company," I suggest.

"Then what?"

"I don't know." I shrug helplessly. "Jack helps Marnie with all kinds of stuff. She likes working with him because my dad trusted him. That's hard to come by in the business world.

People are always looking for ways to take you down and claim your spot. Jack isn't like that. He was perfectly content being the small fish because my dad made him billions. He didn't want the headache that came with being the majority stakeholder."

"What do you think about him?" Rhys leans back against the door, the picture of casual indifference even though the question is anything but. "You trust him?"

"I guess so. He's been kind of like an uncle to me for the last half of my life. We've never been super close or anything, but he's always been nice to me," I say. "I'm glad he's helping Marnie oversee the company. I know I'll have to deal with it sooner or later, but I guess I'm kind of relieved it's not my responsibility yet."

"You don't want it?" Rhys seems surprised.

"It's not that. It's just...I don't know the first thing about running a company." I glance down at my lap, plucking at the tassels on the pillow. "My dream was always music. Maybe that sounds naïve or makes me foolish or whatever, but I never wanted to be a billionaire. I never wanted to inherit my dad's fortune or his company or any of it. I just wanted to sing."

"Chase your dream, songbird."

I glance up at him.

"Life is too fucking short to spend it doing something you hate," he says, his eyes locked on mine. "If you don't want to run the company, don't. Let Jack run it or hire someone to run it for you. Sell it. Set it aside for the baby. You have options and plenty of time to figure it out. Brant wouldn't want you to give up your dream to babysit his."

"What if I want to run it?" I whisper.

"Do you?"

"I don't know. Part of me feels like I need to do it," I admit. "I know you don't agree with what Marnie did, but she wasn't entirely wrong. My dad *did* coddle me. I like to think I'm not a spoiled little rich girl, but the truth is that I *am*. Everything has always been handed to me. Sure, I've worked hard to make sure I earned my spot, but that doesn't change the fact that I had opportunities others didn't. I have no real-world skills. What happens if I fail at singing?"

"You won't fail."

"People fail every day, Rhys. Incredibly talented, deserving people."

"So you're just going to give up?" His eyes narrow, his voice dropping to a growl.

"No, of course not." I shake my head emphatically. "I'm just saying...oh, I don't know what I'm saying!" I groan, tipping my head forward into my hands.

"You're confused."

"No, I'm tired of being poor little Raven," I correct. That's the heart of the problem, isn't it? No one takes me seriously, and why should they? When have I ever given them a reason to take me seriously? "Everyone else makes decisions for me or decides what's best for me because they don't think I'm capable of doing it myself. I'm tired of being infantilized and treated like a child. And that's my fault for allowing it to happen. I let my dad coddle me. I let myself be the spoiled little rich girl. I let myself get to a place where I'm almost twenty-two and have no real-world experience. I put my dream before everything, and this is the result."

Rhys pushes away from the door and strolls toward me. "You aren't a child, songbird. You aren't a spoiled little rich girl. You're allowed to have dreams and throw your heart into them. Your dad didn't spoil you because he thought you weren't strong or capable, he spoiled you because he loved you."

"I know that."

"Do you?" He sits on the ottoman in front of me, putting us at eye level. He's so close that I can see the flecks of gold in his eyes. "Your dad didn't leave you the company to force you into running it. He left the company to you because, out of everyone, he trusted you to make the best decision for the company. He knew you wouldn't be blinded by greed or driven by your own self-interests. When the time comes, you'll make the decision that's best for the company."

He's right, I know he is.

"I feel like I know nothing," I sigh. "I'm tired of being protected from everything."

Tell me what you're keeping from me. Please.

"Brant kept you close because it's so goddamn easy to keep you close," he says, watching me intently. "God, princess. You light up every room you walk into. There's just this innocence about you that people want to protect. We're drawn to your light because it shines like a fucking beacon in the dark."

"Rhys," I whisper, my heart thudding against my ribcage so loudly I'm sure he can hear it.

"We want to preserve it because *we* need it. Because this world needs it. But you don't owe the world anything more than you want to give it. You do enough just by existing. You don't have to prove anything to anyone or be enough for anyone but yourself," he says.

"I want..." I start to utter the confession, swallow it back, and then start again. Once. Twice. I'm like a music track that keeps skipping, caught in the same cycle. I repeat the same snippet, unable to move past it. I want... I want... I want...

"Tell me," Rhys says, freeing me from the loop.

I take a breath and move past the cycle. "I want to be enough for you."

"Fuck," he growls, his pupils flaring. "You think you aren't already? Say the words, and I'll show you how wrong you are."

"I..."

"Say them."

I'm not sure if it's a demand to give him what he wants or a plea to set him free. Either way, I can't resist it. I can't resist *this*. We were both kidding ourselves if we thought we could. We knew the minute he agreed to let me stay here where this would lead.

In the end, it doesn't matter what he's keeping from me.

He's my Kryptonite. I think I might be his too.

"I need you," I whisper, shaking with the profundity of that statement. I *do* need him. Like air or water or hope. I've needed him for three years and have been drowning without him for just as long. He's my port, my anchor, the one damn thing in this world that makes sense to me.

He lifts me off the couch into his lap, his strong arms engulfing me. The pillow lands on the floor beside the ottoman as my legs encircle his waist. I wrap myself around him like a koala bear, clinging like I don't intend to ever let him go. Maybe I won't. Maybe I'll stay right here forever.

His lips land against mine, one hand plunging into my hair to angle my head. Bliss ignites fires in my veins, sending smoke signals straight to heaven. This is what joy feels like. It's his lips against mine, his predatory growl vibrating against my chest. It's his hard body against mine, one hand on my ass. He ruins me with a single kiss, and oh! The pure *ecstasy* of it.

"You taste like sugar, sweet Raven," he mutters against my lips. "I'm not going to be able to keep my mouth off you now."

"Good. Don't," I gasp, running my hands all over his back. His shoulders are so broad. It's strange. I'm tall and curvy, but on his lap, I feel small and dainty. Even though he's beneath me, his sheer size still overwhelms me. *He* overwhelms me in the best way possible.

His tongue tangles with mine, and my mind ceases to function. He's heat and liquid steam, setting off explosions in places I didn't know existed. I thrust my hands into his hair, gasping as my entire body seems to surge to life at the same time, clamoring for attention. My clit throbs, my nipples aching. I squirm on his lap, overwhelmed with the urge to move.

His teeth clamp down around my earlobe. The sting sends a jolt straight to my clit.

"You keep wiggling like that, I'll have you naked in two seconds, songbird," he says against my skin, his voice gritty. "I'm hanging on by a thread here."

"Cut it." I'm not sure where the demand comes from. Years of pent-up desire, maybe. But it comes out powerful, and confident. I'm a mess of competing desires, aching to go places I've never been, but I'm not unsure or hesitant. I made my decision. There is no going back now.

He nips my earlobe again, his stubble scraping deliciously at my skin. His fingers tug at my hair, sending chills throughout my system. His other hand skims across my ass as he grips me hard, holding me in place. "I hope you're ready for me, sweet Raven. You're mine now."

Yes. Oh, God, yes.

Before I can respond, he rakes his teeth down the tendon in my neck. My entire body quivers. A moan rolls from my lips, his name bursting on my tongue in a song of ecstasy. I dig my nails into his skin through his black Friday Harbor police t-shirt, clutching him to me.

"Harder," he grunts. "I want your marks embedded in my skin, princess."

I give him what he wants, digging my fingers into his broad shoulders hard enough to leave indentions. His body is rock solid beneath mine, unyielding. He's hard and hot, the most real thing I've ever touched.

"You were on the beach," he murmurs against my neck. "I can taste the salt on your skin."

"Yes," I gasp. I sang to the ocean today, letting the wind carry my confession out to sea. Rhys hasn't heard my song yet. No one but the waves has heard it. But I wrote it for him. When I sing it Friday, I'll be singing it for him.

"And yet you still taste like sugar." He shifts us, gently laying me out on the ottoman. It's one of those massive square leather ones that run the length of the sofa. I feel like he's laying me out on a bed.

He lands on his knees between my legs, staring up at me in reverence. His green eyes are so dark, so full of mystery and awe, as if I'm the most beautiful thing he's ever seen. With him, I feel that way. He emboldens me, empowers me, and brings me to life in ways I never imagined.

One big hand grips my hip, holding me steady beneath him. The other slides up my leg, starting at my calf. His palm is rough against my bare skin, but it feels like silk too. My skin turns to gooseflesh, reacting to his touch. He notices. His eyes lock on my leg, watching in rapt fascination as he trails his hand higher and the gooseflesh climbs with him.

He stops when he reaches the leg of my shorts. His fingers skim just below the hem, teasing at my inner thigh. He teases at the waistband too, running his thumb back and forth, back and forth. He never goes any higher than my thigh or any lower than my waistband, but somehow manages to make me crazy anyway.

My clit aches and pulses, pleading for attention. Pleading for him.

"Rhys," I moan.

He leans forward and kisses me again. The tip of his tongue dances with mine...teasing there too. He gives me just a little taste. Just enough to make me ache for more. I crave this man with an intensity that's overwhelming.

I'm an addict. Every moment with him makes me need more. Every touch increases my tolerance and requires even more to sustain me. Soon, I'll be completely lost to him. I already feel it happening. And like an addict, I don't care. I just want him. More, more, more. Until he runs through my veins, and I exist on him alone.

Is it the same for him? Does he feel me in the same way?

Is it selfish that I hope he does?

"Please," I moan, pleading for more.

He bites my bottom lip, dragging it between his teeth in a delicious glide.

The sting fades to pleasure as his body comes down over mine. He's so damn big. God, he's a giant. A Titan. He completely engulfs me as the boards in the ottoman groan as if to protest our combined weight.

He breaks our kiss, his lips trailing down my throat. His stubble scrapes my skin as he bites and kisses, driving me higher and higher. My hands slip from his shoulders, exploring down his back. I scratch, dragging my nails down the thick bands of muscle.

He growls his pleasure, crawling over me. His erection grinds against my center. His mouth lands against my right breast.

"Rhys!" I cry out, stunned when he bites me through my shirt. Another sharp pulse goes straight to my clit. I've never felt that before. Ever.

"You like that, don't you?"

"Yes."

He rears back suddenly, reaching for my shirt. Faster than I can process, it's in a heap on the floor. His eyes blaze with intensity as he stares down at me. No one looks at me like he does. No one sees me like he does. Seeing myself in his eyes is beautiful.

"You're going to ruin me," he growls.

"I want to ruin you." I swallow hard, staring up at him. "I want to make you crazy, Rhys."

He growls again, yanking the cups of my bra down. Cool air kisses my nipples and then he's there, pushing them together, burying his face in them. He groans like a man on the brink. One dying and finding salvation in the same breath.

"You already are," he says.

I don't get a chance to respond. He pulls one nipple into his mouth, covering the other with his palm. I cry out in bliss, raking my nails down his back, clutching him to me...vibrating to a frequency I've never heard. Powerful sensations buffet my body, each one shooting straight to my core.

He rocks his hips, grinding his erection against my clit as he gorges himself on my breasts. He's a dichotomy on top of me. Gentle one moment, rough the next. He bites me and then soothes it with a sweet kiss, curses and then tells me how beautiful I am. Holds me like I'm spun glass but grinds against me like I'm unbreakable.

I love it.

"No!" I cry out, reaching for him when he pries himself off me.

"Take your shorts off, sweet Raven," he croons. "Let me see you."

I try to obey, but he yanks his shirt off over his head and I lose the ability to think. I've never seen him shirtless before. The tattoos on his arms are a mere preview of the rest of him. He's covered in them. They climb and coil around his body like living, breathing pieces of him, each one painstakingly etched into his golden skin in vivid color. He is so damn beautiful.

"Shorts off, princess," he growls. "Panties too."

I reach for the button on my shorts, breathing hard. He watches me just as intently as I watch him. It's like we're both caught in thrall, spellbound. I fumble the zipper down and lift my hips to shimmy them down my thighs, taking my panties with them.

Heat climbs into my cheeks as I kick them away, revealing my body to him. He's seen me naked before, but it's different this time. When I got here the other night, I was freezing. Getting naked in front of him wasn't intentional. It wasn't about sex. I was too numb to think about his eyes on my body or if he liked what he saw. My world was collapsing in on itself and nothing else mattered.

Right now, this matters. The look in his eyes matters. The way he groans and grinds his palm against his crotch matters. Part of me thinks I should hide myself from his gaze. That's what a girl my size is supposed to do. Hide my body. Feel shame that I have stretch marks and rolls. That I'm too curvy, too thick. That my stomach isn't flat, and my hips are too wide. That's what we're told we're supposed to feel. Our bodies are supposed to embarrass us. We're supposed to hide them away in shame. But I feel no shame. Not now. Not with him.

I let my legs fall open. I let him look at me.

The look in his eyes...*God, that look.* His eyes are twin flames of forest green, the desire in them scorching me. Burning me alive. He doesn't like my body. He loves it. His tongue skates along his bottom lip as if he's trying to taste me on them. He grinds his palm against his erection again.

"Touch your pussy, songbird. Let me watch."

My hand shakes as I slide it down my body. I don't obey at first. I tease him, running my hand everywhere except where he wants me to touch. I'm not sure why. Something inside guides me, whispering to me to make him wait. To make him crazy.

It doesn't take long.

"Do it," he snarls, fire snapping in his eyes.

He's bossy and impatient. Greedy.

I slip my hand between my legs, parting my folds. I'm so wet it's ridiculous. A loud moan tumbles from my lips as my finger circles my clit. I've barely even touched myself and I'm already on the verge of an orgasm. It's never happened this fast before. I know that's because of him. Because he's here. Because he touched me. Because God help me, I love the thought of this man watching me. How many times have I thought about it? Slipped my hand into my panties and imagined him watching me from the shadows? Too many to count.

I don't know why, but I tell him this.

"I've thought about this," I whisper, spreading my legs wider. "About you watching me." My thumb rolls over my clit, my back arching from the ottoman. "I'd touch myself at night and pretend you were in my room watching me."

"Did you cry out for me, princess?" he asks, his gaze locked on my pussy.

"Yes."

"Did you say my name when you came?"

"Yes," I moan.

"Did you pretend it was my hand working between your legs, Raven? That it was me touching your perfect little cunt?" he asks.

"Yes," I sob. "Every night, I pretended it was you. I wanted it to be you!"

He snaps like a guitar string pulled too tightly. A loud roar leaves his lips and then he's on me. The ottoman scoots across the hardwood floor as he lands between my legs, his mouth against my pussy. He yanks me toward him, pulling my hand out of his way at the same time. I lose the ability to function then.

He eats me like a man pushed too far, one taunted with treats and then told they aren't for him. No one tells Rhys no. He takes what he wants, drinking me down his throat and then coming back for more. Again and again.

I cry out his name as the orgasm rips through me so fast it knocks the breath out of me. An explosion detonates in my core and sets off a landslide in my veins. I melt into nothing and rise from the ashes reformed from pure pleasure. It's too much. Way too much.

"No," he growls when I try to wiggle out from beneath him. He grabs my hands in one of his, easily containing me. "I want one more, Raven. Give it to me." He doesn't even stop what he's doing. He just issues his command between licks, growling it against my pussy.

"I...I..." I try to tell him that I can't, except I quickly discover I *can*. I *am*. The second orgasm builds faster than the first, hotter and more intense. It's going to wreck me. I already know it is. And yet I want it anyway.

He buries his face deeper, working his tongue into my opening. I sob his name as he fucks me with it, thrusting it as deep as he can get it. His filthy sounds fill the living room in a hedonistic, carnal song of gluttony. Mine sings in harmony.

I break wide open for him, convulsing as my orgasm splits me asunder. It flings me around like a buoy in the water just outside the windows, leaving me limp and gasping for breath. He pulls back covered in my juices. They practically drip down his chest.

He doesn't bother taking his pants off. I don't think he can. He rips through the button and zipper in record time, breathing like he just ran a race. His eyes never leave my body. Mine never leave him. Not even as aftershocks wrack my body.

I squeeze my legs together when he pulls his cock out. He's so big. My God. He's going to split me in two. Pre-cum drips from the tip as he wraps a hand around his shaft and squeezes, working himself roughly. Everything about him is rough. Big. Mean. And yet he treats me like I'm precious. No one speaks to me the way he does, says the things he says to me, or looks at me the way he does, as if he finds me worthy of the highest regard. As if I alone touch the heart of him and soften his sharp edges.

"Are you on birth control?" he asks.

I shake my head, a seed of doubt sprouting in my stomach. If he stops now, it'll break me.

"Good," he grunts, satisfaction in his eyes. They run over me, hot and wild. "I don't have condoms, songbird. Haven't been with a woman in years so I haven't needed them." He licks his lips, stepping closer. "Wouldn't wear one with you even if I had one."

My heart leaps into my throat, that little seed of doubt dying as quickly as it bloomed.

He plants one knee on the ottoman between my thighs and then scoops me up, scooting me backward. "I should take you to my bed for this, but fuck if I can wait that long," he mutters, his mouth against my ear. "I need in you now, songbird."

"Then get in me, Rhys," I plead, wrapping my arms around his neck. I hook one leg around his hip, locking my body to his. He could take me on the floor, and I wouldn't complain. When I remember this moment, I'm not going to be disappointed about where it happened. All I care about is that it's him. It's us.

"Lay back."

I reluctantly release my hold on him, falling back against the ottoman. He yanks my ass up into his lap, sliding one hand around my hip. His erection falls against my center, hot and hard. God, he's so damn hard. His other hand slides up my abdomen, between my breasts, and then around my throat. He squeezes gently, heat in his eyes as he tilts my head forward.

"Watch," he orders. "I want you to see the minute I take what's mine, princess."

"Rhys," I moan.

"I want you to see what I do to you."

I groan his name as he releases my throat and grabs his shaft. He toys with me, running it through my folds, bouncing it against my clit. He smacks it against my pussy, closes my lips around it, and jerks himself off with them, grunting curses. It's filthy and fascinating and I can't look away. This is a side of Rhys I've never seen. He's pure sex and sexy as hell.

By the time he lines up at my entrance, I'm writhing beneath him. He's on the edge of breaking but trying to rein it in for my sake. I see it written all over his face. But I don't want gentle Rhys. I don't want him holding back, afraid he's going to hurt me. I want him as wild as he makes me. I want him raw and untamed. I want everything he has.

"Take what's yours, Rhys," I whisper.

"Raven," he growls.

"I saved it for you. All this time, I've been holding onto it for you."

He roars my name...and breaks. He thrusts forward, pushing into me. I feel a brief pinch as my hymen stretches and then tears around him, but the pain is over before it even truly begins, unable to stand in the face of so much pleasure. It crashes down on me from all sides as he thrusts in, not stopping until he's balls deep and I'm stretched to capacity around him. Then and only then does he pause.

His head kicks back, another loud roar ripping from his lips.

I sob his name in ecstasy. He feels so good. So damn good.

And then he starts moving. He doesn't take it slow. He moves like a storm, powerful, fierce. The ottoman rocks beneath us as he pounds into me, fucking me hard and deep. I shout his name, sobbing it into the room.

He falls forward, catching himself on his forearms. His mouth lands against mine, his kiss tinged with so much sweetness it brings tears to my eyes. This man... Lord, I think this man is going to destroy me. And I think I'm going to let him.

"Three years," he whispers against my lips. "Every goddamn minute for three years, you've belonged to me."

I sob my agreement, clawing down his back. I'm not gentle about it. He roars in pain and pleasure, yanking my leg up over his hip. The change in angle allows him to slide deeper. He fucks me harder, as if he's trying to fuck his way into my very soul. I take everything he gives me, moving with him, demanding more. More, more, more.

It'll never be enough. I could overdose on him and still want more, still need more. God help us both, but this isn't the kind of obsession that fades or dies or diminishes. It'll keep growing until it consumes us both or destroys us both. Heaven or hell. Those are the only ways out of this one.

Please be heaven, I pray. *Please.*

Rhys is all over me as he fucks me, kissing me, consuming me. He sets me ablaze again and again. I go up like kindling beneath him, setting him to burn with me. Sweat rolls in rivulets down his abdomen and dampens his hair. He's a work of art above me, one made just for me.

"Rhys!" I cry, nearly catapulting off the ottoman when he slips his hand between us to play with my clit. My entire body clenches, pleasure washing over me in waves.

"Stop fighting it, songbird."

I push him away and pull him closer at the same time, trying to deny the truth. I am fighting it. I don't want this to end.

"Stop fighting it, goddammit," he growls, grinding his thumb against my clit. "Stop fighting me and give me what I want."

I sob his name...and give in. My muscles clamp down on him, fluttering as the orgasm takes me. I shout his name, wailing it into the room. The orgasm hits me like a wall. I forget to breathe, forget my own name as it rips me apart, vicious in its intensity.

Rhys roars my name and goes wild above me. He slams into me without rhythm. Once. Twice. A third time. And then he stills. A long, low groan ripples through the room as he shudders, and then he's coming too. He spills into me in hot splashes, filling me full of him.

"This is nice," I whisper, cuddling up against his chest in the whirlpool bathtub an hour later. He carried me in here as soon as he could move, insisting I soak. He said it'd help. I think he's worried he was too rough with me. He wasn't. I don't regret a second of what we did.

"Yeah?" he asks, trailing his fingers down my back.

"Mmhmm. No one has ever bathed me before."

"I certainly fucking hope not."

I laugh quietly. I love this jealous, possessive side of Rhys. Maybe I shouldn't encourage it, but I love knowing that he doesn't want to share me. I love knowing that he hates the thought of me with anyone else. Thinking about him with other women used to drive me crazy.

"Can I ask you a question?"

"Anything," he says immediately.

"You said it's been years since you were with anyone," I say hesitantly. "How many years?"

"I don't know."

"Oh." I pause. "More than three?"

His hand stills on my back.

My stomach churns.

"Never mind," I whisper, suddenly not so sure I want to hear his answer. "Let's just pretend I didn't ask that question. It's none of my business."

"Raven, look at me."

I stare at the bubbles instead. I shouldn't have asked. Of course, he's been with other women since he met me. Why wouldn't he be? We weren't together. He wasn't mine.

Liar, my mind whispers.

It's not wrong. I hate the thought of him with someone else. I hate that he could be with someone else while claiming that I was his.

He curses beneath his breath and then hooks his finger under my chin, gently forcing me to look at him. I try to resist, but he's implacable. He's a big bully is what he is.

"What?" I say, glaring at him.

"I haven't even thought about touching another woman since the day I met you," he says, holding my gaze. "My goddamn dick hadn't taken much interest in anything for years until you. Then I got one look at you, and he decided it was you or nothing, Raven."

"Oh." I swallow hard.

"Even knowing I couldn't have you, I was faithful to you."

"Rhys," I whisper, feeling about two inches tall. Smaller.

"I don't share and I won't be shared. Does that answer your question?"

I nod.

"You done being mad now?"

I nod again.

He scrutinizes my expression and then shakes his head and chuckles. "Brant always said you were stubborn as all hell," he mutters, tucking me back up against his chest. "Not like he could talk since he was stubborn as shit. But he loved to bitch about how recalcitrant you were."

I smile at that. He did like to complain about me being stubborn. As if I didn't get it from him. He was as hard-headed as they come. No one told him no or got in his way when he wanted something. He'd give you the shirt off his back, but if pushed far enough, he'd dig in his heels out of sheer spite.

He'd be furious if he knew about me and Rhys. I sigh sadly, deflating like a balloon at the thought. Guilt pricks at me, but I push it away. It's too late to take it back now. I'm not even sure I would if I could. My dad was my hero, but he's gone. No amount of wishing will change that or bring him back. But Rhys and I are still here. And we have to pick up the pieces the best we can. Maybe he wouldn't approve of us being together. But I know he would want us to be happy. Rhys makes me happy. Somehow, that has to be enough. It's all I have to offer because I can't live my life for him. I have to live it for me.

I don't want to end up like Marnie, angry at the world and pushing everyone away. If I don't find a way to make peace with my dad's death, that's exactly how I'll end up. I have so much anger inside me over it, so many unanswered questions. But Rhys grounds me. He brings me comfort and happiness. With him, I finally feel like I'm living again.

It has to be enough.

"What are you thinking about, songbird?" Rhys asks.

"Marnie. My dad." I sigh, swirling my hand through the water. "You never did tell me what happened with her the other day."

"We talked. We came to an agreement. The end."

I snort, pretty sure he's editing out a whole lot. "Is she doing okay? Does she look...happy?"

"She's Marnie," he says. "She looks beautiful. Your dad would love to see her carrying his kid."

"Yeah," I whisper.

"She claimed she canceled your cards to help you," he says after a minute. "In her mind, maybe she actually thinks that. Who the fuck knows with her?"

"She was right."

He grunts.

"She was," I say softly.

"She wasn't right about the tuition. She said you lied about that."

"I did not!" I gasp.

"I know."

"I don't understand her. What did I ever do to her to make her hate me so much?" I scowl at the water, genuinely perplexed. "I've never been anything less than nice to her."

"You exist, songbird," he says, rubbing my back. "That's enough for her."

I crane my head back to look at him, surprised by the venom in his voice. "You don't like her, do you?"

"Nope," he says without hesitation.

"Why not?"

"She hurt you."

He's not lying, but he's not telling me the whole truth either. It's another secret. I see it in his eyes. The silent acknowledgment that this goes deeper, that there are entire volumes he isn't saying. That I'm missing entire chapters of subtext. That worries me.

What is he hiding?

What does he know?

More importantly...what does Marnie have to do with my dad's death? Because for the first time, I'm suddenly sure that she's involved. And I think Rhys knows it too.

Chapter Seven

RHYS

"Where are we going?" Raven asks for the tenth time in as many minutes.

"You'll see."

She grumbles under her breath, making me smile. Apparently, she doesn't like surprises. I have a feeling she'll like this one, though. Her performance is the day after tomorrow. She's been working her ass off to get ready, but she won't divulge any details. All I know is that she needs a piano.

"Do you like living on the island?" she asks as we wind our way through downtown. Traffic is heavy, reducing us to a slow crawl. Typical for late evening. I intended to cut out of work early but got stuck working another fucking robbery.

The only thing that annoys me more than drunk tourists are assholes who prey on tourists. They come to the island specifically to pick off unsuspecting tourists. They've been doing it for years. With so many out-of-towners concentrated in one area, they can hold up a tourist and then slip into the crowd and disappear.

This idiot didn't check for cameras. We've got his ugly mug front and center on a couple of security cameras. We printed off the photos and sent them to the docks. Once he tries to leave the island, he'll be in cuffs.

"Usually," I say. "Traffic is a pain in the ass."

Raven makes a face at me. She's been quiet since we talked about Marnie last night, lost in her own thoughts. Truth is, I have been too. I've been lying to myself, believing I could hold her close and keep the truth from her at the same time. I can't. She deserves to know everything. I'm an asshole for touching her without confessing to what I've done.

I'll burn in hell for that.

But the pieces are finally coming together. I think I'm finally beginning to understand what I've been missing all along. I know what Marnie is after. I think I even know why she killed Brant. Before I tell Raven the truth, I need to ensure that I'm right. If I am, it changes everything. If I'm not, I lose her for good. I'm balanced on the blade of a fucking sword.

Nothing justifies the choices I made, and I know that. But I made them for her. Because God help me, there's not a fucking thing in this world I wouldn't do for her. I don't merely love her. That word isn't strong enough for what beats in my chest for her. My soul is hers. I gave it into her keeping long ago.

I pull into the church parking lot and kill the engine.

"You're taking me to church?" She eyes me sideways. "I'm not dressed for church, Rhys!"

"Songbird, it's an island," I say with a chuckle. "We don't get fancy for church. Besides, you look beautiful." She does. Her dark tresses are pulled back from her face by a purple headband that matches her purple and white sundress. She's fresh-faced, her nose pink from the sun. "But there is no service here tonight. The place is only open for services on Sundays. The rest of the week, islanders use it for gatherings or meetings."

"Oh." She breathes a sigh of relief. "What kind of gathering?"

"A private one." I smile and pocket the keys before climbing out of the truck. A stiff breeze blows in from the Sound, rustling through the treetops. Seagulls scream overhead, their cries mingling with the sounds of traffic and the voices carrying from restaurant patios. Friday Harbor is never quiet at this time of day.

I circle around the truck and open Raven's door, helping her down. I shouldn't do it, but I slide her down my body, gritting my teeth when my cock immediately stiffens in my pants. Keeping my hands off her is an exercise in futility, but I'm trying like hell to behave. She needs a break. I was rough with her last night.

I couldn't stay out of her this morning either. She slept in my bed where she belongs, her naked ass nestled against my cock. I ate her for breakfast and then fucked her as the sun rose. Thought about calling in to stay in bed and do it again, but knew if I didn't leave the house, she'd be too sore to move today.

She stumbles into me, her breathing choppy when her feet finally touch the ground. She has stars in her eyes. I love that look on her face, as if she thinks I'm something special, something mighty. Does she know she could fell me with a single word?

"Come on," I growl, determined to get her inside before I lose the willpower to do it at all.

We walk hand in hand to the church.

"You have a key to a church?" she asks, wide-eyed when I pull it from my pocket to unlock the side door.

"I'm a cop."

"Oh, yeah."

I chuckle, shaking my head. "Got tired of waking the pastor up in the middle of the night every time we had to come and deal with another break-in, so he had keys made for me and Rodrigo."

"People break into churches?" The horror in her voice is the cutest thing I've ever heard.

"Afraid so, princess," I say. Churches get broken into frequently. People think they keep cash lying around. When they can't find that, they grab laptops, gift cards...whatever they can carry. Criminals are criminals even in houses of worship.

"Wow," she mumbles, shaking her head like she's completely disappointed in the human race.

I flip the lights on and lead her into the sanctuary. The church is small, with a center aisle and a dozen pews on each side. An organ sits at the right side of the stage up front, a grand piano on the left. I lace our fingers together and pull her up the aisle toward the piano.

"This is why we're here, songbird."

"Oh," she whispers, reaching out to trail her fingers along the keys. And then she snatches it back at the last second and peeks around. "Are you sure it's okay?"

"I cleared it with the pastor. You have permission to practice here right up until the show on Friday," I say, handing the key to her with a flourish.

"Seriously?" She gapes between me and the key.

"Seriously. It's all yours, sweet Raven."

She squeaks and flings herself at my chest. I catch her, dropping the key in the process. It bounces against the wooded floor at our feet. Somehow, she ends up in my arms, my hands on her ass. Our lips crash together, our kiss hot and heavy.

I dive in again and again, drinking from her lips like she's wine. My hands rove all over her ass, squeezing, kneading...doing things they damn well shouldn't be doing in the middle of a church. Christ, not even Jesus could blame me for this. She's too sweet.

I reluctantly break the kiss, pressing my forehead to hers with a groan. "You keep kissing me like that, we'll be doing a whole lot of things in this church that aren't sanctioned by Pastor Bob or the Holy Spirit, sweet Raven."

She laughs softly, the sound full of happiness. My stomach clenches, my cock throbbing. Does she have any idea what she does to me? How wild I am about her?

"No way," she says, squirming for me to put her down. "I need to get into heaven."

"Yeah? Why is that?"

She beams at me over her shoulder, her blue eyes bright. "It's where you're going."

"What's up, my man?" Michael Kincaid asks. "You bored as fuck on your little island and ready to come work for the big boys yet?"

"Nope," I say, grinning. Kincaid works for the DEA's gang unit in Seattle. He's a chameleon, the last person you'd expect to be as smart as he is, and yet he knows everything there is to know about gangs and gang crime. He's been shot, stabbed, and left for dead more than once, but they never manage to kill him. When you need info, he's the guy you call. He can find out anything about anyone. He's the scariest motherfucker I know. Criminals with brains respect him. Those without sense quickly learn to fear him. "Hell will freeze over before I come work with your crazy ass, brother."

"Well, fuck you too then," he says, laughing. "I could use a little begging in my life today. *Kincaid, please save me before my nuts shrivel up and I die of boredom* sounds like a good start."

"No can do, fucker."

"Fine. Then why are you blowing up my phone at ass o'clock on a Thursday?"

"I need a favor."

"Does it have the potential to get me shot? Because, gotta say, man, been there, done that. Kinda getting old," he says. "The big boss is riding my dick about giving me a partner. So if whatever you need help with has a likelihood of making that happen, my answer is probably no."

"Only probably?" I lean back in my chair, planting one boot on my desk.

"I mean...if it's going to piss him off, I might be in," he mutters, making me laugh.

Kincaid has spent most of his life living with gangs and criminals. He never takes anything seriously...and yet he closes more cases than most other agents. He's a beast. I don't know what his story is, but he's a closed book. He doesn't share shit and doesn't ask shit.

"It probably won't get you shot," I say. "But it may get me fired."

"Damn." He whistles. "Now you've got me curious as a motherfucker."

"I know who killed Brantley Calloway. I've known for a while. The only thing I'm missing is the why," I say, not lying to him.

"Who?"

"His wife."

Kincaid whistles again.

"She claims it was an accident, but I'm not buying it," I say and then fill him in on the whole sordid story. I don't leave anything out. If he's going to look into this, he needs to know everything. Is it a risk? Yes. But it's one I have to take. As soon as I start pulling threads, the whole goddamn thing is going to collapse on my head. Kincaid won't have that problem. He knows people who know people.

"Jesus Christ, Flannery," he says. "If a goddamn dumpster fire and a shitshow had a baby, and then that baby got together with a bomb and had baby, that kid would still be less fucked up than your situation."

"I know."

"You think he's really working with the mob?"

"No. I think Jack Hale is," I say. "And I think Marnie's carrying his kid." It's the only thing that makes sense. Jack was the piece of the puzzle that I was missing. I think Brant knew the kid didn't belong to him the minute Marnie told him she was pregnant. He probably threatened to leave her. Only she and Jack couldn't risk losing control of the company, so they cooked up a plan to involve me.

She claimed he was the one working for the mob. Marnie fucking knew I'd leap to protect Raven. As soon as she had me where she wanted me, she killed Brant. With him out of the way, she and Jack had control of the company. All she had to do was keep me quiet and keep Raven out of the picture until the baby was born. At that point, Brant would be listed on the birth certificate since they were married when the baby was conceived, and she'd be home free. The courts would split the majority share of the company between Raven and the baby, leaving Jack with the controlling interest. The company would be theirs.

She fucked up, though. I would never have had a reason to suspect Jack had she not tried to keep Raven from graduating. She tipped her hand and fucked herself over. They weren't in a business meeting when I went to see her. He didn't look at her like a business associate. He looked at her like a man in love, one frustrated by a woman playing games.

He hated that I was there. As if I'd touch the bitch with a ten-foot pole. She's pure poison. I don't know when she and Jack started hooking up and I don't want to know. All I want is to watch them both burn. They deserve everything they get. If I go up in flames with them, fuck it. At least I'll take the two of them with me.

I owe Raven that much. I owe it to Brant too.

"Goddamn," Kincaid says when I tell him my theory. "What the fuck is it with rich people? They'll never be able to spend what they already have, but they're still so fucking desperate for more. They'll destroy their own flesh and blood and not even bat a lash."

"Hell if I know," I mutter.

"I don't have many mob connections, but I know a few people who should be able to help," he says. "I'll see what I can find out and get back to you." He pauses. "I'm guessing you need me to hurry it the fuck up?"

"That'd be nice."

He grunts. "Does this island of yours have boats and shit?"

"It's an island."

"Right."

I laugh quietly. Why am I not surprised Kincaid hasn't stepped foot on one of the islands? He probably hasn't ever left the city. I don't think he ever takes a day off, truthfully.

"Consider me invited."

"You help me bring them down, I'll take you out on my boat."

"Cool." He pauses. "I'm not going fucking fishing, man."

"Call me when you find something."

"Flannery, I'm serious. I'm not fucking fishing!" he shouts.

I disconnect, dropping my phone on my desk. For a moment, I just sit there, staring blankly into space. Having the truth out there feels...different. Like a weight has been lifted. I've been carrying it for too long.

That was the easy part, though. The hard part is still to come.

That's the part I might not survive.

Chapter Eight

RAVEN

My pulse pounds, nervous energy pumping through me. The bar is packed. They're loud and boisterous, cheering on the act ahead of me. I peek my head out from backstage, scanning for Rhys. He's late. Is he coming?

My stomach churns with anxiety.

I haven't seen him since he dropped me off at the church this morning. He had lunch delivered for me. I hoped he'd swing by to eat with me, but he didn't. He's been radio silent today. It's...unnerving. I'm not sure what's going on, but I don't like it.

I consider switching my song and playing it safe.

The thought lasts all of two seconds.

I played it safe for three years. I'm not doing that anymore. I'm leaving my soul out on that stage for him tonight. Heaven or hell. It has to be one or the other.

"Five minutes," the stage manager says, holding up five fingers to make sure I heard him loud and clear. He's the same guy who was at the door when I came in the other day. I think his name is Joe. Or John. Or Jason. I don't remember.

I nod, letting him know I'll be ready.

"You look beautiful."

A hand slides around my waist.

"Rhys." I melt into him, my knees weakening with relief. He's here. He came. "You're here."

"Wouldn't miss it for the world, songbird," he says, planting his lips against the side of my throat. He runs them up to my ear. "I've been waiting to hear you sing since the first time I heard you speak. You're going to blow them all away."

The only one I want to blow away is him.

"Are you nervous?"

"No." Now that he's here, I'm not nervous at all.

"Good." He nips my earlobe. "I'll be right here waiting for you, princess. I know Brant will be too. Go make him proud."

I spin around and hug him tightly. "Thank you," I whisper, my throat welling with emotion.

"For what?"

"For being you."

"Two minutes, Raven!" Jason, his name is definitely Jason, says.

Rhys brushes his lips across my forehead and gently sets me away from him. "Sing, songbird."

I nod and hurry toward the stage, blocking out everything except the notes. I run through the lyrics in my head and see the piano arrangement behind my eyes. My breathing is controlled, exactly the way I was taught.

The act before me—a young girl strumming a guitar—finishes her song. It's a fun island ditty that has everyone clapping along. A few people are up dancing. Everyone claps and cheers when Tawnie hops up on the stage with her. Two waitresses appear with buckets, circulating through the crowd. People drop in money as they pass by.

The girl waves, blows a kiss, and then bounds off the stage.

"Break a leg!" she says, a genuine smile on her face as she passes by me.

"Thank you."

Tawnie introduces me.

I take one last look over my shoulder at Rhys and step out onto the stage. It's bright and loud. I wave. Smile. Everyone claps, their energy high. I slide onto the piano bench. My hands are steady as I place them on the keys.

The crowd quiets, the dull roar fading.

I take a breath...and sing.

I said I could live without you
That I didn't need to breathe
Until I found myself in your arms
Illusion shatters quickly when truth settles in

Because I've been lying to myself
Crying to myself
Pretending you aren't all I need
But, baby, I'm broken for you
Hoping you've been needing me too

Unmasked and stripped of all pretenses
Not whole without you, but bound to you
Begging you, begging you
Choose me too

Because I've been lying to myself
Crying to myself
Pretending you aren't all I need
But, baby, I'm broken for you
Hoping you've been needing me too

Please, love me too.

A heavy silence permeates the bar. The only sound is the blood rushing in a thick hum through my veins and the final, mournful strains of my song as it fades to a whisper. My chest barely rises, my breaths shallow. I keep my eyes closed, waiting for the final note of the song to fade.

I feel Rhys watching me from the shadows, his gaze heavy. It sets me on fire, making me ache for him. Always, I ache for him.

I take another shallow breath and release it. It seems unnaturally loud in the deafening silence around me.

No one moves.

Five seconds tick by.

Ten.

Fifteen.

Thunderous applause erupts from every corner of the room, as deafening as the silence that preceded it. Triumph blooms in my chest, relief. I poured my whole soul into that song, and they loved it.

I rise to my feet. Tawnie hops up on stage, beaming at me. I don't hear what she says. My mind is focused entirely on Rhys. As soon as the buckets come out, I spin and rush off the stage, eager to get to him, to share this moment with him.

As soon as he sees me coming toward him, he opens his arms, ready to catch me. I crash into him like a meteor, knocking him back a little deeper into the shadows. His body engulfs me, his breathing ragged. His erection presses against my belly. All I see in the dark are his green eyes blazing with unholy fire.

"Jesus, Raven," he growls.

Our lips meet, our tongues moving in a perfectly choreographed dance. We melt into one another, a tangle of trembling limbs and greedy desperation. Of forbidden desire and helpless addiction. We're slaves to it, unable to deny the strength of the bond between us.

He's my father's best friend, but that's not what I think about when he touches me. All I think about is how good he is to me, and how badly I ache for him. All I see is him, that big body hewn from one thick slab of muscle. Those tattoos painted across his golden skin. The angular cut of his jaw and the full, uneven lips that kiss me like he plans to survive off me.

"You sing like a fucking angel," he whispers, breaking the kiss to look at me. His expression is aswirl with emotion. Pride. Possession. Desire.

Does he know I sang for him? That I meant every word?

"I missed you today," I whisper instead of telling him.

"Yeah?" he asks.

I bob my head, strands of my hair catching on the wooden wall. We're completely hidden from the rest of the bar, tucked in an alcove behind the stage. They're only yards away, but miles might as well separate us. They're muted, their applause fading as Tawnie introduces the next act for the night.

"Were you singing for me, sweet Raven?" Rhys asks, his firm hands locking down on my hips.

"I..."

"Don't lie to me, songbird."

"Yes," I whisper.

He grunts his satisfaction, pulling me closer. I feel the hard ridge of his erection against my belly. Anticipation turns my nipples to hard points. We're in the middle of a bar, and I want him anyway. I think some part of me wants him right now *because* we're in the middle of a bar. There's a naughty, forbidden edge to the desire coursing through my veins. I know he won't allow anyone to see me. But the thought that they're so close...I like it.

"Rhys? I need you."

A growl rumbles in his throat.

"Please," I whisper, feeling like I might spiral out of control. I've never thought about having sex like this, with one hundred other people so close. But I'm not surprised. When Rhys touches me, nothing else matters. He consumes me, turns me into some wanton version of myself that I find myself eager to know. She's braver than I am, bolder. Capable of keeping this dark prince worshipping at her feet.

"You need to come, Raven?" he asks, spinning me around in his arms so I'm staring out at the stage. His hand splays across my belly, so low I feel the heat of it between my legs. "You want me inside you right here?"

I moan his name.

"Tell me," he demands, pressing his lips to my exposed shoulder. His hand creeps lower.

Warmth rushes through me, every nerve ending in my body firing.

"Tell me, Raven."

"Yes." The word is a mere whisper of sound exhaled into the shadows.

"No, princess. I want you to say the words. Open that sweet mouth and tell me what you want me to do to you."

"I..." I falter and then reach deep for a little courage. "Fuck me, Rhys. Please."

He spins me to face him again, his forest eyes twin flames of male satisfaction.

"Kiss me," he demands, thrusting his hand into my hair to crane my head back.

I kiss him willingly, my lips whispering along his before I slip my tongue inside his mouth, emboldened the way I always am in his arms. I pour everything into the kiss, trying to wreck him like he always does me. Warmth turns to heat and then to fire and liquid flame. It licks along every inch of my skin, turning need into a painful, blistering ache.

"I need you."

I'm not sure which of us speaks those words. I feel his need for me as if it's my own. He feels mine the same way, I know he does. We feed off each other, our desire creating a powerful harmonic that flows between us in an unbroken line. First in me and then in him. When he's kissing me, I feel every second, every heartbeat.

I lose myself in it, reveling in the euphoria it sends bubbling through my veins.

Music swells to life around us, so loud I feel it vibrating in my stomach and my chest. It doesn't stop us, doesn't pull us apart. We drown in bliss together, locked in a passionate embrace, caught in the notes of forever. He rucks my dress up, his rough hand gliding up my thigh. I tug at his pants, trying to free his cock.

Cool air dances against my inner thighs and then my damp panties.

He doesn't stop kissing me. Not even when I wrap my fingers around his hard length, stroking him the way he taught me. He likes it rough, likes a little bit of pain with his pleasure. I give it to him, reminding him of how good I can be for him.

"Jesus," he growls, shoving his hand inside my panties.

The only thing that saves the whole bar from hearing my cry of ecstasy is his mouth against mine. He claims that sound for himself, drinking it down his eager throat as he twists his wrist, thrusting two fingers into me. I rise up on my tiptoes as he fucks me with them, ruthlessly dragging me to the edge with two fingers inside me and his thumb on my clit.

"When I get you home, we're going to do this again, Raven," he says, dragging my bottom lip through his teeth. "I'm going to leave my seed dripping from both of these pretty little holes tonight."

"Yes," I sob, uncaring if anyone hears me. Willing to give him whatever he wants. It's all his anyway, claimed the second he wrapped his hand around my throat and demanded I watch him take what belonged to him. He's filthy and demanding...and so damn *good*. God, the way he takes care of me makes me feel like I really am his princess, worshipped and adored by him.

He fucks me with his fingers until my legs quiver. I faceplant into his shoulder, biting him as I come around his fingers in a warm rush of pleasure that liquefies my veins.

"Good girl," he croons. "Don't let anyone hear you coming all over your man or I won't let you do it again."

My man. More like my heart. My soul. My everything.

Does he know how much I need him? How much I love him?

I release his skin from between my teeth, biting my lip to keep from crying out for him. I know he isn't joking. If anyone hears me, he won't let me come again. He'll keep me on the edge all night, tormenting me with pleasure until I beg for mercy. The sexy, bossy bastard. He wasn't joking when he said he wouldn't share me. He's jealous and possessive. And I love every second of it.

"Touch me, Raven," he orders, pulling his hand out of my panties to lick my juices from his fingers. He holds my gaze the whole time, making sure I see him doing it. Making sure I know how much he likes the way I taste. "Stroke my cock."

I give him what he wants, of course. Touching him is my favorite thing to do. Seeing the pleasure in his eyes, hearing it in each harshly panted breath. Watching his upper lip curl and his body quiver in response to my touch.... When I die, I want him to be the last thing I see. I want him to be the last thing I remember.

He's hard silk in my hand, heavy and burning hot.

"Ah, God, baby girl," he groans, writhing beneath my touch.

I smile, pleased by his reaction. He never hides the way he feels when I touch him. And no matter how many times I touch him, his reaction is always the same. There is no shame, no guilt. He doesn't worry about what my father would say if he were still alive. He's completely mine in these moments, as much a slave to his carnal need as I am.

I work his cock slowly, squeezing and releasing in time to the strains of music spilling out around us. He rocks his hips in the same rhythm, rising and falling as if compelled to follow the stroke of my hand.

"I want you, Rhys," I whisper, dancing my fingertips across his balls.

"You have me." He takes a step away from me so his dick falls from my hand. Even then, it stands at attention, pointing right toward me. He spins me around again, maneuvering me until my hands are against the wall, my hips canted back with my ass in the air.

"So sexy," he growls, yanking my dress up. My panties are pushed to the side. And then he's right there again, playing with me from behind, driving me crazy again. He doesn't thrust into me, though. He teases me, mercilessly dragging me closer to another orgasm.

When I'm on the edge again, biting my cheek to keep from screaming a plea, he finally takes pity on me. He fills me in one hard thrust, not stopping until his hips are flush with my ass and I'm writhing on his cock. In pleasure. In pain. He's so damn big. Every time he's in me, I forget how to breathe.

He grunts, reveling in that first deep thrust and in how it feels to be connected again. He engulfs me as his body bows over mine. One hand tangles with mine against the wall, pinning me in place. His lips ghost across the back of my neck in silent, reverent prayer. My body erupts in chills, the kind I feel everywhere.

"You keep letting me in you bare, you'll be carrying my kid soon, Raven," he says.

I hear the desire in his voice, the ache. My own rises to meet it, just as poignant, just as powerful. I'd give this gorgeous man fifteen babies if he asked it of me, and I'd love every second of it.

"Don't let anyone hear you," he whispers.

He fucks me in slow, deep thrusts, pushing forward until the tip of his dick is against my cervix and then rocking back to do it all over again. He stays bent over me, keeping me pinned in place, my cheek against the rough, cool wood. When I turn my head slightly, I see the crowded bar. People move in flashes and flickers, no more than small parts of them visible—an arm here, the side of a face there.

Somehow, Rhys knows I'm watching them. Somehow, he knows *me*. Every naughty, wanton thought in my head, every forbidden desire. Nothing is secret from him. Whether that's because he's a detective or because I'm an open book, I don't know. But I love it.

"Do you think any of them know what I'm doing to you back here, princess?" he asks.

"Rhys," I moan, too turned on to think straight.

"Do you think they know how good you feel wrapped around my cock?" He nips my ear and then soothes it with his tongue.

"I..."

"They'll never know how good you feel," he growls, jealous and territorial. I don't have to ask to know how he'd react if anyone saw us together like this. He'd flip this bar upside down in rage. And yet he gives me this anyway because I wanted it. Because he always gives me exactly what I want, even when doing it drives him crazy. "You're mine."

His gritty words grind against my insides, shaking loose a desperation I've never felt before. I want to belong to this man, more than I want anything. I'm so in love with him. I don't know how I'm supposed to leave him when summer ends. I can't. I *know* I can't.

"You'll always be mine, Raven," he growls in my ear, still tormenting me with those slow thrusts. "No one else will ever touch you like this or *fuck* you like this. No one. This body is mine."

"Rhys," I cry, writhing against the wall. He's ruining me with his words. With his breath in my ear. With his cock buried inside me.

"I heard your song, princess," he says, releasing my hand where it's pinned against the wall to plunge his into my hair. He cranes my head back, pulling just enough to make it sting. His mouth lands against the side of my cheek, his breath a harsh pant. "You think I don't feel the same way? That I wouldn't kill for you?"

"Rhys," I sob, my heart jumping into my throat. He means it; I know he does.

"You're my soul, songbird. You hear me? *You're my soul.*"

For the first time since my dad died, I know joy. It rips through me with the force of a hurricane. Everything grows brighter, the weight that's been on my chest for days dissolving into nothing.

I truly get lost then, in him. In love. In the storm raging through me, threatening to unmake me at the cellular level.

"I'll never give you up," he whispers, his lips against mine. "Not ever."

"Don't stop," I sob, dancing that line between ecstasy and outright rapture.

He doesn't stop. He grips my hip, holding me still as he picks up the pace, pounding into me. He fucks me hard, knocking me breathless with every hard thrust. And still, it's not enough for me. Not hard enough, not deep enough. I'm greedy when it comes to him, always wanting more, always needing more.

"I hope I do get you pregnant. Right here and right now."

A sob builds in my throat as sensation begins to overwhelm me, pushing me closer to that line where life and death meet. I cry out his name as the line snaps and I vibrate apart, spiraling into another dimension. An explosion of color dances behind my eyelids, pulsing in time to the music around us, to the grind of his hips against mine, to the beat of his heart against my back.

"God, yeah, Raven," he groans. "I feel you coming all over me. You like soaking my cock, princess?"

"Yes," I sob, not lying. Nothing has ever felt better than I do when I'm coming with him deep inside me.

His grip on my hip tightens, my name leaving his lips on a moan.

I squeeze my inner muscles, trying to pull him over the edge with me.

It works.

"Jesus," he growls. He thrusts deep and stills, holding me hard as his cock pulses inside me.

As soon as I feel him coming inside me, I come apart again, helpless to stop it. In this moment, we're not two disparate people, unalike in every way. He's not my dad's best friend. He isn't keeping secrets and I'm not leaving for Boston at the end of the summer. Nothing between us is complicated or fragile. We're not Rhys and Raven, but one powerful being, locked in ecstasy and drowning together. In this moment, the only thing that matters is this...*us.*

I slump against the wall as the waves slowly retreat.

"Please don't let me go," I whisper, vulnerable in a way I have never been before. Exposed in a way I have never been before. I'm not asking for him to hold me now, but to hold me forever. To stay inside me, holding me together for the rest of my life and whatever comes after. I think I may need him that long. I *know* I'll love him that long.

"Never," he vows, pressing his lips to mine. "Never, princess."

I think he means it.

God, I hope he means it. Because when summer ends...I don't think I can leave him.

"I love you, songbird."

I gasp as his soft confession reaches my ears and overflows my heart. Tears spill down my cheeks. I was wrong earlier. This is joy.

"I love you," he whispers again.

"Take me home, Rhys," I demand, needing to be alone with him. I don't care about the contest anymore. I don't care about the job. Everything I care about is right here.

Chapter Nine

RAVEN

"Wake up, songbird," Rhys whispers, his hand drifting down my side.

I groan, rolling away from him. "It's too early."

"I know." His lips brush my naked shoulder. "There was an incident out at one of the farms. I have to go."

I crack one eye open. The bedroom is still dark, light barely peeking over the horizon outside. It's not even fully dawn yet. Way too early. "What kind of incident?"

"A shooting," he says with a sigh. "Looks like it was self-inflicted, but I have to go check it out."

"Okay," I whisper, wishing he didn't have to go. He didn't get much sleep last night. Neither of us did. We made love over and over. The things he did to me...the things I did to *him*. When I die, I want those memories to be the last things that play through my mind. Every muscle in my body is deliciously sore. I'm exhausted. It's perfect. Perfect.

"I love you."

"I love you too."

"Get some sleep. I'll be home as soon as I can," he says, brushing his lips across my forehead.

"'Kay."

The bed dips...and then I'm out.

My phone wakes me up at a little after eleven.

"Hello?" I mumble, not even looking to see who it is.

"Raven? It's Tawnie."

"Oh." I sit bolt upright in the bed, the blankets falling from around me. "Hi."

"You wowed everyone last night," she says. "They're still talking about you this morning."

"Really?"

"You snuck out before I could give you the tips you made last night," she says with a laugh. "Not that I blame you. I didn't realize you're dating Detective Flannery."

"Um..." Am I supposed to tell people we're dating? We haven't exactly been discreet, have we? "Yes, he's mine," I say, deciding I'm not going to hide it. We've been hiding for too damn long already. I can't do that anymore.

"Good for you," she says with a laugh. "He's a good man."

"The best," I whisper.

"If you want to swing by this weekend, I have your tips for you. And we can discuss your availability. Obviously, you stole the whole show."

"What? Seriously? I won?" I gape in shock.

"You won." She laughs. "I'm pretty sure half of the other performers voted for you."

"Oh, wow."

"Swing by this weekend and we'll talk."

"I will. Thank you so much!"

I disconnect and then jump up from the bed and squeal, dancing around the room like a crazy person. I can't believe I actually won the slot in the schedule.

A childish part of me wants to rub it in Marnie's face. I've tried to give her the benefit of the doubt, but I think Rhys is right. She didn't do anything to help me. She did everything to hurt me. She hates me because my dad loved me, and nothing I do will ever change the way she feels about me. So I'm not going to try. I'm going to celebrate my success with the man I love and leave her out of it.

Holy crap. I won. I actually have a job now.

"Ouch," I mutter, careening into Rhys's desk mid-happy dance. My feet come out from beneath me and I land in a heap on the floor. I flop onto my back and laugh loudly, glad he wasn't here to see that. He'd probably lose his mind.

My gaze catches on a file sticking out from beneath his desk. It's tucked between the reinforcement boards and the shelf where his laptop sits as if he intended to hide it there. I stare at it for a long moment, trying to figure out why he'd hide a file when he lives alone, and then realization dawns. He hid it from me.

It's my dad's file.

I sit up, my heart thumping against my ribcage. Without even thinking about it, I reach for it. My hand closes around the thick file, plucking it from its hiding place. Then and only then do I pause. Whatever he knows is in this file. Whatever he's hiding is in here.

My mind and heart briefly war. One says to put it back and wait. To trust that he'll tell me. The other says that I have a right to know. That this is *my* father. That side wins. Not because I don't trust Rhys, but because *this is my father*. I promised I wouldn't go looking for answers and I've kept my promise. But when the answers are in my hands, I can't put them back and pretend I don't have a right to know.

I open the file.

The first thing that falls out is a stack of photos. I immediately set those aside without even looking at them. I've seen enough true crime to know I don't want to see what they contain. Some images, you can't erase. I don't need to see crime scene photos or my dad lying on the floor. I don't need to see the autopsy photos. I want my memories to be full of him laughing and smiling, of the crinkles around his blue eyes and the humor that always glinted in them.

I also set the autopsy report aside. I know what killed him. Blunt force trauma to the head. Skull fractures. Whoever attacked him knocked him over the coffee table. He landed on his back, his head cracking against the stone fireplace. All so they could take a couple of thousand dollars from his office, a handgun, a Rolex he never wore, and some of Marnie's jewelry.

I set the police report aside too. I've already read it front to back. It's been splashed all over the news. There's nothing there that I don't already know. The whole world knows what it contains.

The next sheaf of papers confuses me. They're about the company, but I don't understand what they mean. Financial documents with notes jotted in the margins, newspaper articles on mergers and acquisitions. There are several about Marcellus Moretti.

I know that name. Everyone knows Marcellus Moretti's name. He's a mobster in New York, one of the biggest there is. At least that's what everyone says. Why is his name mixed up with my dad's case? Does Rhys think he has something to do with my dad's death?

His warning about not being able to unknow things floats to the surface of my mind.

Everyone has secrets, songbird.

I shiver and set aside the articles about Marcellus Moretti. If Rhys thinks my dad was tangled up with him, he's wrong. My dad would never get involved with a man like him, not ever. I may not know everything about him, but I know that much.

The only other thing in the file is a notebook. I pick it up and flip through, finding page after page of Rhys's notes. He writes in tiny, bold print. It's masculine and elegant at the same time. Scooping everything back into the file, I climb to my feet and carry it into the bathroom with me. I set it on the counter and take care of business.

Once I'm done, I pick it up and carry it back to the bedroom with me before sitting down in his desk chair to read through the notebook. The first few pages don't tell me much. I don't even understand half of it. They're written in some police speak that reads like a foreign language.

And then I get to the timeline. I scan through it, a helpless witness to a trainwreck. I know I should stop and look away, and yet I can't. It gets worse and worse, the wreckage piling up. My stomach heaves as I finally understand what Rhys has been trying so hard to protect me from. My instinct was right the other day.

Marnie killed my dad.

But I was wrong too.

There was never a choice between heaven and hell for me and Rhys. There was never a choice at all. It was always hell for us. It was always destruction. Because he knew she did it. From the very beginning, he knew.

"Oh God," I cry, my stomach heaving. I leap up from the chair, toppling it backward as I rush into the bathroom.

I land on my knees beside the toilet, collapsing as my heart shatters. As everything shatters. And I break.

I leave everything at Rhys's. My phone, my clothes. Everything except the case file. I grab it, throw on a dress, and leave. I stop by the bar long enough to pick up my tips, promising Tawnie that I'll come back later to discuss my schedule. She knows something is wrong.

She asks me five different times if I'm okay.

I don't even answer her the last time. I just stumble out, headed for the ferry. I have to get off the island before Rhys comes looking for me. Before he realizes that I know everything. It's not raining this time, thank God.

I manage to rush on at the last minute and make my way up to the passenger deck. It's crowded this time. I curl up in the corner and stare out the window. Tears slip down my cheeks, but I don't make a sound. I don't breathe until the ferry pushes away from the island, leaving Rhys far behind.

I don't go to the police. Not yet. I go to Seattle.

The taxi pulls up in front of my dad's house a little after six. He eyes me speculatively, no doubt hoping for a big tip. I push a bunch of bills in his direction, not even looking at them. It should cover the trip from Anacortes and his tip.

He pulls away before I even have both feet on the ground.

I march up the steps, my heart pounding. I'm running on pure adrenaline. Pure rage. But I want to look Marnie in the eyes and ask her why. I want her to explain it to me. Why did she take my dad from me? Why does she hate me? What gives her the right to play the grieving widow when she's the reason he's gone?

"Raven," she says as soon as she throws the door open. She doesn't look surprised to see me. Did Rhys call her? Does he know I found his file?

Of course he called her. He probably warned her that I know.

My heart screams in protest. It bleeds. God, it hurts.

"You killed my dad."

Her eyes widen in shock.

"You killed my dad!" I scream. And then I'm crying again, sobbing so hard I can't breathe.

"Come inside," Marnie says, grabbing my arm.

I'm too damn miserable to argue. I'm too damn miserable to do anything but follow along like a broken little doll as she pulls me into the house. As soon as she does, I realize just how badly I messed up. Because she isn't alone. Jack Hale is here, and he has a gun.

He's pointing it right at me.

Chapter Ten

RHYS

"Yo, Flannery!"

I stop walking and turn as Rodrigo shouts my name from across the parking lot.

"Tawnie McAllister just called. She said your girl was just at her place ten minutes ago," he says, jogging toward me. "Said she looked like she'd seen a ghost. She thought you'd want to know."

What the fuck?

I frown, instantly worried. I already know Raven won the contest last night, so I know that's not the problem. Four different people have brought it up today. They wanted to know when she'd be singing again. I'm proud as hell of her. She sang like a fucking angel last night. I've never heard anything like her before. There's no way I'm letting her run Brant's company. I'll quit the force and do it myself before I let her give up her dream. She was born to be on stage.

"Thanks," I mutter to Rodrigo, jogging to my truck. I fish my phone out of my pocket and dial her number. After the fourth ring, it sends me to voicemail. "Call me when you get this, songbird." I disconnect and shoot her a text before hopping in the truck.

I'd hoped to be home by now, but paperwork is a bitch. There's always a ream of it when it comes to gun deaths, and Jonas Reamer's wasn't pleasant. He didn't mean to kill himself, but guns and alcohol never mix. He was showing off and accidentally shot himself. His family is broken up over it. We had to interview everyone who was out there and go through the whole scene. It took a while.

I pull out of the parking lot and head toward the house, keeping an eye out for Raven along the way. By the time I pull into the driveway, I haven't seen her. She hasn't answered her phone either. I hit the garage door button and pull in.

"Raven?" I shout as soon as I'm over the threshold, but I know immediately that she isn't here. I can sense her when she is. It's as if she's a piece of me, connected to me on some level that goes beyond the physical. I check through every room anyway, my worry intensifying when I find my desk chair toppled over and her phone on the bed. She never leaves the house without it.

I scroll through it, looking for any hint of what might have upset her. Aside from my calls, the only other one she got today came from the bar. Something is wrong. Seriously fucking wrong.

My instincts are screaming that truth at me.

I pace toward the desk, the air leaving my lungs in a rush when I see a photo on the floor beside the chair. It's one of her and Brant, the same one I've taken out of the case file a thousand times and looked at.

The case file.

I drop to my knees, reaching beneath the desk for the file.

It's gone. She knows.

Where is she?

Horror rushes through me, chilling me to the bone as the answer immediately materializes.

No. Please, God, no.

But I already know I'm right. I *know* her.

She went to confront Marnie.

I leap to my feet and take off, running full-out through the house, my heart in my throat.

"Flannery," Kincaid says as soon as the plane touches down at the airfield just outside of Seattle and my feet are on the ground. His steely blue-gray eyes are grim, his lips pursed. His shield hangs around his neck on a chain, dangling over the bulletproof plate on his vest. He's covered in tattoos with a piercing in his eyebrow. Even dressed like a cop, he looks like a gangster. There's something wild in his eyes, something dangerous. He isn't tame. He never will be.

"Tell me she's safe," I rasp.

"Seattle PD has eyes on the house."

It's not an answer and we both know it. My knees threaten to buckle, but somehow, I manage to keep myself upright. I manage to keep moving. I don't walk. I jog to the SUV waiting for me a few yards away.

Another man in a DEA vest waits inside.

"Ames, this is Flannery, Flannery, this is Jason Ames," Kincaid says, introducing us.

I jerk my chin in a nod of greeting. I've never met him before, but I know of him. He's the Assistant Special Agent in Charge of the DEA in Seattle. He's one of the youngest in the country. He's also one of the most well-respected. If he's here, it's not good.

"Tell me," I growl as soon as Kincaid and I are both in the vehicle.

"Your girl is at the house," Kincaid says.

Fuck, princess. Why? Why didn't you come to me?

But I already know the answer to that question, don't I? Why would she come to me? I had every opportunity to tell her the truth, but I didn't. I stalled. I put it off. I waited. I couldn't fucking stand the thought of watching the light in her eyes die. Of seeing her look at me with revulsion.

She needs me, but she's the reason I fucking *breathe*. I wanted to hang onto her love for as long as I could. When it comes to her, I'm a selfish motherfucker.

"I have worse news, brother," Kincaid says, his voice soft, apologetic.

"Tell me," I grit out.

"Jack Hale arrived at the house about half an hour before she did," he says. "They've got the blinds closed so we can't see what's going on inside, but she was screaming at the pregnant chick about killing her dad when the pregnant chick pulled her inside."

"Jesus Christ," I breathe, my stomach twisting itself into knots. This is my fault. All of it.

Kincaid blows out a breath. "And you were right. Jack is in deep with Marcellus Moretti. I don't know what you did to piss him off, but he does not like you," he says as Ames pulls out, headed toward Seattle. "As soon as I started digging, my sources started getting skittish."

"Fuck. He knows," I mutter, thumping my head against the seat. Jack knew the gig was up as soon as I saw them together. He had to know I'd figure it out. Marnie may be impulsive and driven by spite, but Jack isn't. He's been laundering money through Brant's company for years without being found out, and he managed to do it in a way that incriminated the hell out of Brant. He's smart and crafty. A real wily motherfucker.

"Yeah, I'm thinking he does," Kincaid agrees. "And I'm guessing he'll use her to get to you now that he has her. You need to decide how you want to play this."

There is no decision to make. If it's my life or hers, she lives. It's the only outcome that I can accept. A life without her isn't a life anyway. It's a death sentence. But if I die, I'm taking that motherfucker with me. He won't ever get near her again.

"I'm going in after her," I say, my voice grim.

Ames glances at me in the rearview mirror. "We need whatever evidence you have before you go in," he says. "If things go south, we're going to need it."

"I'll make whatever statement you need me to make," I say. "But the only evidence I have is in that house with Raven. She took the case file with her when she left today."

"Ames, you might as well get my goddamn workers comp shit started," Kincaid says with a resigned sigh. "I'm probably getting shot again today."

"If I have to do more fucking paperwork, I'm shooting you myself, Kincaid." He looks at me again, his expression firm but not unkind. He's a hard-ass, but he goes to bat for the people who deserve it. If he's here now, it's because he's decided I deserve it. I don't know why. I'm not looking that gift horse in the mouth. I'll take whatever help I can get right now. "Don't fucking die in there or I'm going to be pissed."

"Don't plan on it," I growl.

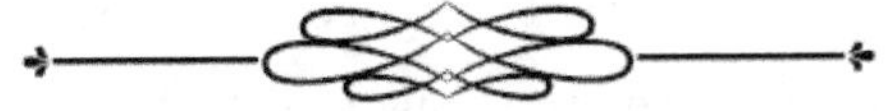

I give my statement on the way, laying it all out for Ames. I don't ask what he thinks, and he doesn't tell me. Right now, it doesn't matter. The only thing that matters is Raven. If I go down, I go down. It is what it is. So long as she's safe, I'll live with it.

Seattle PD has the street cordoned off a block from Brant's. It's a fucking jungle of cop cars and SWAT vans. The DEA and FBI are both here. It's Seattle's case, but no one gainsays Ames when he takes command of the scene. When you're the biggest fish in the pond, you call the shots.

Kincaid fills everyone in on the scope of the situation. A murmur of unease goes through the crowd when he informs them that we're going in solo. No one likes that much.

"Why are we sending in the man who helped cover up the crime?" a blond DEA agent mutters.

"You mean the man who solved the goddamn crime?" Ames asks, his hard gaze cracking through the crowd. "Without him, Marnie Calloway would be in prison for murder, Brant Calloway would have taken the fall for the money laundering, and the FBI wouldn't have a RICO case against Jack Hale and Marcellus Moretti right now. Moretti would have a multi-billionaire dollar company in his control, and every other man standing here would have allowed it to happen."

The DEA agent who spoke up shifts uncomfortably. No one else says anything.

"Being a cop isn't about doing the easy thing," Ames says. "It's about doing the right thing, even when it's the difficult thing. Flannery risked everything to protect the people who deserved to be protected. That's the oath we take. That's the line we hold. He upheld his at great personal cost to himself. In case you've forgotten, Brant Calloway was his friend. And the woman he loves is inside that house now. We're given discretion for a reason. He used his to achieve the best possible outcome. You don't have to like his methods. You don't have to agree with them. But I expect you to stow your shit and get on board or get off my goddamn scene."

For a full five count, no one says anything. No one leaves either.

"It was just a question," the DEA agent mutters then.

"It was a stupid fucking question," Kincaid retorts.

"House is always asking stupid fucking questions," Tito Alvarez, an old friend from Seattle PD says, earning chuckles from a few other officers.

I glance at Tito, who lifts his chin in a nod. At least everyone here isn't out for my blood.

"I'm surprised you can hear my questions over the sound of your girl screaming my name," House says, flipping Tito off. He pitches his voice high, mimicking the sound of a woman's voice. "Ricky. Ricky. Oh, Ricky! You're so much bigger than Tito."

"Alright, settle down," Ames barks, rolling his eyes when everyone laughs. "We don't have time for this bullshit."

He's right. We don't. I'm ready to go get my girl.

I'm coming, songbird. I swear, I'm coming for you. Just hang on.

Chapter Eleven

RAVEN

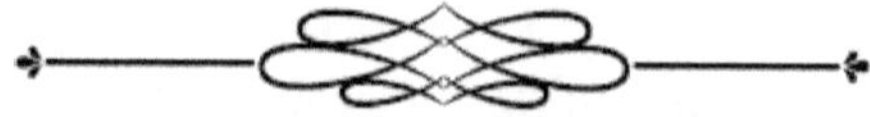

"Jack, put the damn gun down!" Marnie cries, stomping her foot. "She's not going anywhere. Look at her." She flings a hand in my direction. "You have her tied to a chair for Christ's sake."

Jack flicks his gaze in my direction from his seat at the poker table and then takes another sip of brandy. He ignores Marnie's demand...just like he's been doing for the last hour and a half. I gave up pleading an hour ago, but she keeps on. It's obvious he isn't going to listen. I'm not even sure why she's trying.

Out of the two of them, she's the one who hates me. If anyone should be pointing a gun at me, it should be her. Funny how I don't even know who the real enemy is in my life. Everyone I trusted has been lying to me, manipulating me, using me. Marnie wants me gone. Jack wants my dad's company. And Rhys...I don't know what Rhys wants. I don't care what he wants.

Liar, liar pants on fire, a little voice whispers.

I push it down, refusing to listen to it.

"For the love of God," Marnie says.

"Oh, shut up!" I cry. "Just shut up!"

She snaps her mouth closed, looking at me in complete shock. She actually has the audacity to look hurt.

"He isn't putting the gun down. He's going to sit there and drink his brandy and point the damn gun at me until I give him the company, or he's drunk enough to shoot me," I growl. "You yelling at him isn't going to change his mind. He made it up long before I ever walked through the front door. And frankly, if I'm going to die today, I'd rather not die listening to you screech."

Marnie blanches.

Jack chuckles.

"You killed my dad. The only thing I want to hear from you is why. Unless you're telling me that, just shut the hell up!" I shout, too tired to be reasonable. Too exhausted to care. I've never hated anyone before but right now, I hate her. I hate her so much.

She's taken everything from me. My dad. Rhys. Everything.

"It was an accident, Raven," Marnie says, wringing her hands together. "He was laundering money through the company. When I confronted him about it, he got angry. He threatened to take the baby. He tried to grab me. I pushed him and he fell over the coffee table." She cries without tears, sobbing with dry eyes. "I didn't mean for it to happen!"

"You're a liar."

"I'm not lying!" she cries. "I loved your dad. I still love him."

"No, you don't. If you did, you wouldn't be able to stand here and lie about him like that," I growl, yanking at the tape binding me to the chair. It doesn't move. I think they used a whole roll. "He would never launder money through the company, and you know it. He would never grab you or try to hurt you. He *worshipped* you."

"No," she says, switching from tears to sneering so fast it's startling. "He worshipped *you*. All he talked about was *you*. It was always Raven this and Raven that. I could never compete with you!"

I gape at her, incredulous. "Are you kidding me right now? It was never a competition, Marnie! He was your husband. He was my dad. We weren't in competition for his affection or his love. He had enough for both of us. When he came to visit me, all he talked about was you. He loved talking about you because he loved you and he wanted me to love you just as much. That's who he was. He talked about the people he loved because to him, they were his world. *We* were his world."

"Rhys took one look at you and fell head over heels."

"You're in love with Rhys?" I feel like I'm going to throw up.

"God no. I can't stand him." She scrunches up her face and shudders in revulsion. "But everyone loves you, Raven. They fall all over themselves to be close to you. Your dad would drop everything to rush to your side. Rhys would give up everything for you. You have no idea the things he's done for you. I could never compete with that. Even when you weren't here, the whole world revolved around you."

"I *never* wanted the world to revolve around me."

"I did!" she cries. "I wanted it to revolve around me. Just once, I wanted to come first to Brant. Just once, I wanted him to love me as much as I love him. Just once, I wanted to be the one he dropped everything to come running for. But it was always you. When your mom died, he left me alone for *weeks*."

I stare at her, taken aback. I've always known that Marnie was self-absorbed. But I never knew how callous and heartless she was until today. I never knew how cruel she was until today. My mom died, and all she cared about was that my dad left her alone to be there for me. She hates me because my dad was a good dad.

She killed him because he was a good father. There's something so inherently wrong with that, something so twisted and *fucked up* that there are no words for it. I thought coming here would give me answers, but there are no answers. There's just...nothing. My dad didn't die because of anything he did to her. He died because she is who she is. Because she's so fundamentally broken that love is a weapon to her, something you wield to exert control.

I was wrong. I don't hate her. I can't. I *pity* her.

"You're not raising my sibling," I say. "If Jack doesn't kill me today, I'm taking him or her from you. You aren't capable of raising a child. You aren't capable of loving one."

Jack laughs suddenly. "Do you want to tell her, or should I?"

Marnie spins to face him.

"Come on, it'll be fun," he says, a bitter, mocking smile on his face.

"Don't," she whispers.

But he doesn't have to say it. I'm not blind. I can see what's right in front of me. The baby isn't my dad's. It's Jack's. He's in love with her. And he just listened to her pour her heart out about my dad. That has to sting.

I don't feel sorry for him in the slightest. Probably because he's been holding me at gunpoint for the last hour and a half. It's not exactly giving me warm and fuzzy feelings about him.

"Why not?" he asks her, setting his brandy aside. The glass is empty. Half the bottle is empty. "It's not like she's going to survive the day anyway. That is your plan, isn't it? Have poor old Jack blow her head off, leaving you and the baby everything."

"What?" Marnie gasps. "No, of course not."

A movement in the hallway catches my attention. I subtly shift my gaze that way, trying not to draw attention to it. My heart leaps into my throat when I see Rhys standing in the shadows. His eyes connect with mine.

My soul cries out for him.

Even now, I love him. I don't know what that says about me, but it's true.

He lifts his finger to his lips, warning me to be quiet.

I blink, hoping he knows that means I understand, and then slowly shift my gaze back to Marnie and Jack. They're still arguing. Marnie's rambling, trying to convince Jack that her plan is his plan...whatever his plan is. I'm not too clear on that. All

I know is that it involves killing me. Probably Rhys too. Who knows at this point?

They deserve each other. I hope they rot in prison together.

"Then why not tell her?" Jack says, his eyes locked on Marnie.

"She's been through enough, Jack," Marnie says, her voice soft. For the first time, I detect a hint of...guilt. As if she actually regrets her choices. Maybe she does. But it didn't stop her from making them. "Can't that be enough? Please?"

Jack eyes her for a moment and then gives in. He leans back in his chair. When he does, his gaze shifts toward the hallway. I know the minute he spots Rhys in the shadows. His eyes widen in surprise, and he lifts the gun.

The next moment, all hell breaks loose.

Marnie screams as an explosion detonates and smoke rapidly fills the room. A shot rings out and then another. Something flings my chair to the floor. No, not something. Someone. *Rhys.* He dives on top of me, covering me with his body as Jack starts shooting.

"Stay down, songbird," he whispers in my ear. "Stay down."

The next minute, he's gone, prying himself off me.

I struggle against the tape, trying to fight my way free of the chair, choking on the noxious fumes filling the room. It burns my throat, making me gag. Marnie is still screaming. Someone is cursing. Jack? Rhys? I don't know. I hear someone land a blow and then glass shatters.

"Reach for the sky, motherfucker!" an unfamiliar voice booms and then. "Oh, shit."

Another shot rings out.

The room goes silent.

"Rhys?" I scream. "Rhys! Rhys!" I lunge against the tape holding me hostage, desperately trying to free myself to get to Rhys. He has to be okay. He has to be okay. Please, God. Please. *"Rhys!"*

He appears like a mirage, falling to his knees beside me.

I sob his name, so weak with relief I nearly black out.

"I'm here," he says, cupping my face between his palms. "I'm right here."

"I thought... I thought..."

"I know. I'm here." He picks me up, chair and all, and rises to his feet. "Don't look, songbird. Don't look," he croons, burying my face in his shoulder.

I don't look. I don't have to look. I can hear Marnie sobbing brokenly. I know Jack is dead.

"Kincaid, find me some fucking scissors!" Rhys roars, carrying me out of the house into the fresh air. He sets my chair down on the front lawn. Sirens wail, red and blue lights ripping apart the night. It's chaos, but all I see is Rhys.

He sinks to his knees in front of me, pressing his face to my chest. "I thought I lost you. Christ, I thought I lost you," he groans, his whole body shuddering.

For a minute there, I thought I lost myself. I thought I lost *him*.

"I'm right here," I whisper, tears of forgiveness falling down my face. "I'm right here."

Chapter Twelve

RHYS

"Hey," Raven whispers, turning to face me when I walk through the front door. She's standing in front of the windows, a blanket wrapped tightly around her. Despite everything she's been through lately, she's still the most beautiful woman I've ever seen.

"Hey." I drop my keys on the credenza and lean back against the front door, wary. It's been four days since I killed Jack. Four days of endless interviews and questions. So far, I'm not in jail. I have Ames to thank for that. So far, the Sheriff on San Juan isn't firing me. I have Brant to thank for that. Unless the tides turn, it looks like I may actually escape without going to prison.

Marnie wasn't so lucky. She's in jail on first-degree homicide charges. She confessed everything. She's working with the FBI to build a case against Marcellus Moretti. It won't win her any favors. She's still going to prison for a long time. But at least she's doing the right thing for once in her life.

Raven is...quiet. Distant. She's lost in her own mind, and I can't reach her. It's fucking killing me. Seeing her taped to that fucking chair...listening to her screaming for me. If I could bring Jack back and kill him again, I would.

She hasn't been sleeping much. Neither have I. I lie awake at night, just listening to her breathing. Thanking God that she's still with me. That she still lets me hold her and take care of her. We haven't talked much about what I did. We haven't talked much at all. I've been trying to give her time to let everything settle in her mind.

We haven't gone back to the island yet. We're not staying at Brant's either. We're at my old place. I still have it. I'm not giving it up unless they pry it from my cold, dead fingers. Finding real estate in Seattle is a bitch.

"How did today go?" she asks.

I blow out a breath and push away from the door, strolling across the living room toward her. "Come here," I say, holding out my hand for her. She slips hers into mine, letting me pull her into my arms. She doesn't melt into me like she used to, but she doesn't pull away.

I lead her to the couch and sit, pulling her down beside me.

"They're holding her without bail," I say.

She exhales a tiny breath of relief, a little of the weight falling from her shoulders. "That's good," she whispers. And then a cloud passes across her face. "Rhys?"

"Yeah, songbird?"

"What's going to happen to the baby?" she asks.

I want to lie to her, but I can't. "Because Marnie has no family, once she gives birth, the baby will go into the system," I say quietly. "The state will place him or her with a foster family until an adoptive family can be found."

"What if they can't find one?"

"Then he or she will remain a ward of the state."

Raven flinches.

"If that happens, it's not on you, princess," I remind her. "You are a victim in this situation. You didn't create this situation. You have no responsibility in this situation. Marnie and Jack are the ones responsible here. No one else."

"I know," she says. "But..."

"But what?"

"But Marnie and my dad were still married when the baby was conceived. In the eyes of the law, that makes the baby his until DNA says otherwise," she says. "So technically, I'm the baby's next of kin."

"What are you saying?" I ask, watching her carefully.

She's quiet for a long moment. "I guess I'm saying that the baby doesn't deserve to suffer," she finally says. "It's not the baby's fault that his or her parents did horrible things." She bites her lip, looking at me with wide, somber eyes. "I think...I think we should raise the baby, Rhys. It's what my dad would want."

I stare at her. Just stare.

"Jesus," I finally growl, pulling her into my lap to kiss her hard on the mouth. I spear my hand into her hair, angling her head. Her lips part beneath mine on a soft moan. I kiss her long and deep, again and again. Fuck, I missed kissing her.

"What was that for?" she whispers when I finally break away.

"For being you," I say, tucking her hair behind her ear and pulling her up against my chest. "For having a heart as pure as yours. For loving like you do."

"Oh." She cuddles up against me with a sweet sigh. "I've missed you."

"I've been right here, princess."

"I know. I just…"

"Had to decide if I was worth it?"

"What?" She scrambles up, turning those big blue eyes on me. "Is that what you think I've been doing?"

"I wouldn't blame you if it was, Raven. What I did…" I trail off, shaking my head. "I wouldn't blame you if you hated me for it."

"I could never hate you," she whispers vehemently. "I was hurt, and I was angry. It felt like my soul was being ripped out of my body, but I *never* hated you, Rhys."

"I'm sorry, songbird. I'm so fucking sorry for hurting you."

"Promise me that you'll never keep something like that from me again," she demands. "I can't go through that again, Rhys. It hurt so damn bad." Tears well in her eyes, residual pain darkening them. "I couldn't breathe."

I groan, pulling her close. "Never again," I vow. "Never again. I was going to tell you everything, but I was a fucking coward. I kept putting it off, terrified you'd hate me once you knew. You should know the only reason I did what I did was to protect you and Brant and the baby," I murmur. "I know that doesn't make it right. It doesn't earn me forgiveness or make me deserving of it. I know that. But when she came to me threatening to tell the world that he was laundering money through the company, the FBI would seize every single one of his assets. You'd lose everything. Including the image of the man you idolized. I couldn't let that happen."

"I know," she whispers and then swallows hard. "Marnie told me that you risked everything for me, that you did what you did because of me. I don't think she said it to help your case. She kind of hates you. But she hates me more. She told me because she wanted me to know just how much she hates me."

"She's a bitch."

"I thought so too," she says, frowning sadly. "But the truth is, she's just someone completely incapable of love. She doesn't understand that it isn't selfish or shallow. To her, love is a weapon. That's all it will ever be."

"She can rot in prison," I grunt.

"Promise me that we won't let the baby go into the system," she demands.

"If you want to raise the baby, I'll move heaven and earth to make it happen, songbird."

"You don't mind?"

"Brant loved her," I say simply.

Raven smiles, the first smile she's given me in days.

"You're smiling." I brush my thumb across her lips. "I missed that."

"I've been thinking."

"I know. I've been worried as hell about you," I admit.

"I'm sorry," she whispers, guilt in her voice. "I just needed time to put it all together in my mind and make a few decisions."

"What decisions, songbird?"

"About the baby, for one. And about the company." She expels a breath. "I'm going to sell it. You were right about why my dad left it to me. He trusted me to make the best decision for the company, and the best decision is to let it go. It brought him joy, but I don't think I'll ever be able to look at it the way he did. I'll never be able to look at it without all of this tainting it in my mind. And if I can't love it as much as he did, it should go to someone who can."

"He'd probably agree with you, princess," I murmur. "He wouldn't want you tethered to something that brings you pain. If that's all it is to you, let it go."

She nods, wiping tears from beneath her eyes. "I also made a decision about school."

"You're finishing school," I growl.

"I am," she says. "But I'm not doing it at Berklee. At least not in Boston."

"Explain."

"I'm going to switch to online classes to complete my degree." She bites her lip and looks up at me through her lashes. "Hopefully from the island."

"Is this you asking to move in with me?" I ask, amused. Hopeful. Praying.

"Yes," she whispers. "I'll cook and clean. And I have a job now." She scrunches up her nose. "At least I think I still have a job."

"Oh, you definitely have a job," I growl.

"You talked to Tawnie?"

"No."

"Then how do you know I still have a job?"

"Because I'm not talking about the bar."

"Oh. Then what?"

"Being my wife, songbird."

She gapes at me, her mouth open in an adorable little O.

"If you're moving in, you're marrying me," I say, laying her out on the couch beneath me and crawling over her. "Don't care if it's tomorrow or next year, but you're going to be my wife."

"Do I get a say?" she asks.

"Depends on if you're saying yes."

She wraps her arms around my neck, pulling me down to her. "Yes," she whispers in my ear. "Yes, Rhys."

"Fuck," I breathe, every muscle in my body relaxing at once. I tilt my head to the side, sealing her vow the only way I know how. With my lips on hers and my hands on her body. By the time I let her up for air, we're both naked and she's writhing beneath me.

"Rhys," she whispers, staring up at me with that look I've missed so much. The one that says she's mine in every way. "I love you."

"Songbird," I groan, sheathing myself inside her. "Sing us to heaven."

She does. As sweetly as ever.

Epilogue

RAVEN

FIVE YEARS LATER

"Mama, a cow!" Brant says, pointing at one of the hundred cows in the field. "A cow!"

"Moo," our youngest, Gretchen, shouts.

I shake my head and laugh quietly. Our babies always love when we come to visit Cassia and Cord on the ranch. They run around like tiny crazy people, driving the ranch hands nuts. Luckily, the ranch hands are used to it. Cassia and Cord's brood are just as wild as mine.

"Mama." Willow, our oldest, tugs on the hem of my shirt.

"Yeah, sweetheart?"

"I think that cow is running away," she whispers, pointing across the field.

I turn to look and laugh again. "That cow is definitely running away," I say, watching as Patty slips through the fence and makes a beeline for the woods on the far side. She and one of the bulls here, Hamburger, are escape artists. They keep Cassia and Cord on their toes.

"Your cow is escaping again," I tell my sister-in-law.

She looks up from her burger and groans. "Darn it. Cord!" she shouts. "Your cow is on the lam again."

Cord whips around, spatula in hand, automatically homing in on Patty. "That one isn't mine, pretty baby. She's your hellion."

Cassia makes a face at him. "Nope. When I have food, she's yours."

He chuckles and shakes his dark head, his eyes alight with humor. Cord is crazy about my sister-in-law. He'd chase the cow all over this mountain if it made her happy. I'm pretty sure he's actually chased the cow all over this mountain for her more than once.

"Man the grill," he says, handing the spatula to Rhys. "I gotta go find someone to catch the damn cow again."

"You need to buy them some fucking cones like the vet uses," Rhys mutters. "They couldn't slip through the fence then."

"We tried that once. It didn't work." Cord jogs toward the barn, a gaggle of little kids following in his wake. They love the giant cowboy. He's so patient with them. He and Rhys love to give each other hell, but they're a lot alike.

"They make cones big enough for cows?" Rhys asks his sister, flipping a burger.

"Cord had to engineer one." Cassia giggles. "Hamburger destroyed it in fifteen minutes."

Willow snuggles up beside me, laying her head against my arm.

"You okay, sweetheart? You didn't want to go to the barn with the rest of the kids?"

"Nu-huh." She smiles up at me. "I just wanted to sit with you, mama."

My heart melts. I swear, she's the sweetest little girl. If there's any of Marnie in her, I don't see it. She's been with us since the day she was born. Marnie didn't object to us adopting her. I think she knew that Willow would be better off with us than with anyone else.

Willow knows she has another mom. Marnie sends her cards, and they talk on the phone. Rhys took her to see Marnie a couple of times when she was a baby, but Marnie asked him not to bring her anymore. We all agree that's for the best, at least for now. A prison is no place for a little girl, and seeing her didn't help Marnie any. It sent her spiraling into a deep depression. Being able to see your child but never able to touch them has to be hard.

My feelings for Marnie are still conflicted. I don't hate her. I don't wish her any ill will. But I haven't forgiven her either. She murdered my dad and tried to steal his company out of spite. He loved her wildly, and she destroyed him. I don't know if I'll ever be able to forgive her for that. But I am grateful to her. Because of her, I have one of the biggest blessings in my life. My oldest daughter.

I've talked it out a thousand times in therapy and with Rhys, and I've learned to be okay with the way I feel. I've learned to be okay with being conflicted. We're allowed to feel the way we feel. No one has all the answers. We just do the best we can and take it one day at a time.

Most days are good days. Rhys and I are stronger than ever. The way he loves me is indescribable. In his arms, I'm indestructible. He's my safe place and my powder keg, the thing that grounds me and the one person on this planet that ignites me. After five years, I still want him as desperately as ever. I still ache and burn for him.

He still splits my world asunder with a touch. We survived hell and made our own heaven. We carved it out of the wreckage on a little island off the coast of Washington and filled it with babies. I still sing. Sometimes on the island, sometimes on stages around the world. I've had offers for record deals, but I didn't sign any of them. I struck out on my own and did things on my own terms. I work with the producers I want to work with and make the music I want to make.

I'm not a superstar, but I never wanted to be. I just wanted to sing. And I have. But that's not my only dream. Not anymore. Rhys is my dream now. Our babies are my dream now. The life we've built for ourselves is my dream now. It's not full of glitz and glamour, but it's perfect.

Our kids don't know that we're billionaires. Some day when they're old enough, we'll tell them. They'll inherit everything. But we don't need it to be rich. We have each other. We have heaven. We have Cassia, Cord, Rhys's parents, and a small tribe of friends.

It's more than enough.

I think if my dad is looking down on us, he'd be proud.

I think he might even be okay with the fact that we ended up together. Rhys might not be who he would have chosen for me, but not even he could deny that there is no one else in this world who loves me better than his best friend.

"What are you thinking about?" Rhys asks, coming up behind me and wrapping an arm around my shoulders.

I lean against him and tilt my head back, letting the warm rays of the sun spill across my face. "My dad," I say, smiling. "And you."

"Yeah?" He runs his hand down the side of my face. "What about us?"

"I was just thinking that he's probably relieved that I chose you," I say for his ears alone. "Look at the life and the love you've given me. That's all he ever wanted for me. If he's watching, I think he's smiling, knowing two of the people he loves most found it together."

"Jesus." Rhys's hand falls still on my cheek.

"He's at peace now, Rhys," I whisper. "If there was anything to forgive, I think he did it a long time ago. He'd be proud of you, you know. *I'm* proud of you."

"Willow, baby girl? I need you to scoot over for a minute," Rhys says, his eyes locked on mine, emotion blazing in their depths.

Willow obediently slides over.

As soon as she does, Rhys picks me up off the bench and spins me around. His mouth crashes down on mine, his kiss hot and hard. I weave my hands into his hair, holding him to me as he pours his devotion and pride into me, his heart pounding against my breasts.

"I love you, songbird," he breathes against my lips.

"Forever," I whisper back.

Author's Note

IF YOU ENJOYED BEACH House Beauty, please consider leaving a review! I appreciate them so much!

Want more steamy reads from me? Check out Wrecked, the first book in the Ruined Trilogy!

Romancing the Cowboy

"Excuse me?" Cassia sits upright behind me. "T-told me? I don't know you."

I turn to face her, wondering what the hell she's playing at. Surely she remembers calling me a video game-playing basement dweller? The way she avoids looking directly at me tells me plain as day that she remembers me just fine. She just doesn't want me to know that.

"I'm a cattle thief," she blurts before I can sort out why.

"You're a cattle thief?" I blink down at her, trying not to laugh in her face. If she's a cattle thief, I'm a fucking ballerina. Why am I smiling so hard? Better question, why the hell couldn't her friend pick a better day to camp out at Cam's? I need him here to deal with...*everything* so I can carry this sassy little thing upstairs and plant my kid in her.

"Yes. A cattle thief. You should call the police and have me arrested."

"Right." I chuckle, running a palm over the top of my head. The only time she'll be going near the police station is when she's bypassing it on the way to the courthouse to marry me. But I don't tell her that. I'm guessing by the panic in her voice, she doesn't want me to know who she is. Until I figure out why, I'll play her little game. But we're playing it by my rules. "Well, come on then, little cattle thief. Let's go."

"Oh, good, you believe me," she says, her shoulders sagging with relief.

"Any reason I shouldn't?"

"Nope, none at all." She beams at me, smiling so brightly the heavens part and angels actually fucking sing. My cock and heart throb, the blood in my veins resonating in time to that heavenly chorus. I've never been a religious man, but something about this wild woman has me ready to drop to my knees and praise Jesus.

Instead, I watch as she rolls to her knees. She tips her head back, her pretty eyes crawling up my body. I don't imagine the way they go glassy or the heat that steals across her round cheeks. Nor do I imagine the pink tip of her tongue darting out to wet her bottom lip.

"You're naked."

"Not yet," I say, grinning ear to ear. "But I'm willing to change that for you, princess."

She scowls at me. "I mean you're half naked. It's winter. Wear clothes."

"Tore my shirt."

"How? Hulking out of it?"

Romancing the Cowboy is now available!

Wrecked

ONE LOOK AT HIS curvy captive and this Mafia boss will risk it all. Even if it means toppling his own kingdom to the ground...

Rafe Valentino

A life in chains was the deal I made with my father to win my twin's freedom.

My soul is black with the things I've done to keep my promise.

I never regretted any of it until now. Until her.

Amalia Santiago's bravado and fierce defiance make me feel alive in a way I never expected.

I was never meant to fall for her.

I don't deserve to put my filthy hands all over her pristine body.

She's supposed to be my prisoner.

But now, she'll become my world instead.

Amalia Santiago

When the devil came for my foster brother, I let him take me in his place.

I swore I'd find a way out of this mess for both of us.

Except Rafe Valentino wasn't supposed to have a heart...

And I wasn't supposed to fall for the ruthless crime boss.

So why do I come alive when he touches me?

Now, I'm one wrong move from destroying everything.

And nothing is what it seems.

How do I sacrifice the man I love to save my brother?

If you enjoy OTT possessive older men with a little bit of darkness in them and sassy, curvy heroines with heart, get ready to fall for Rafe and Amalia in this sweet and extra steamy romance. As always, Nichole Rose books come complete with a guaranteed HEA. Safe read. No cliffhanger. Each book in the Ruined Trilogy features a different Valentino brother and can be read as a standalone story.

Wrecked is now available.

Instalove Book Club

The Instalove Book Club is now in session!

Get the inside scoop from your favorite instalove authors, meet new authors to love, and snag freebies and bonus content from featured authors every month. The Instalove Book Club newsletter goes out once per week!

Join now to get your hands on bonus scenes and brand-new, exclusive content from our first six featured authors.

Join the Club: http://instaloveinstalovebookclub.com

Nichole's Book Beauties

Want to connect with Nichole and other readers? We're building a girl gang! Join Nichole Rose's Book Beauties on Facebook for fun, games, and behind-the-scenes exclusives!

Follow Nichole

Sign-up for Nichole's mailing list at http://authornicholero se.com/newsletter to stay up to date on all new releases and for exclusive ARC giveaways from Nichole Rose.

Want to connect with Nichole and other readers? Join Nichole Rose's Book Beauties on Facebook!

f

facebook.com/AuthorNicholeRose/

instagram.com/AuthorNicholeRose

twitter.com/AuthNicholeRose

bookbub.com/authors/nichole-rose

tiktok.com/@authornicholerose

More By Nichole Rose

<u>Her Alpha Series</u>

Her Alpha Daddy Next Door

Her Alpha Boss Undercover

Her Alpha's Secret Baby

Her Alpha Protector

Her Date with an Alpha

Her Alpha: The Complete Series

<u>Her Bride Series</u>

His Future Bride

His Stolen Bride

His Secret Bride

His Curvy Bride

His Captive Bride

His Blushing Bride

His Bride: The Complete Series

<u>Claimed Series</u>

Possessing Liberty

Teaching Rowan

Claiming Caroline

Kissing Kennedy

Claimed: The Complete Series

<u>Love on the Clock Series</u>

Adore You

Hold You

Keep You

Protect You

Love on the Clock: The Complete Series

<u>The Billionaires' Club</u>

The Billionaire's Big Bold Weakness

The Billionaire's Big Bold Wish

The Billionaire's Big Bold Woman

The Billionaire's Big Bold Wonder

<u>Playing for Keeps</u>

Cutie Pie

Ice Breaker

Ice Prince

Ice Giant

The Second Generation

A Blushing Bride for Christmas

Love Bites

Come Undone

Dripping Pearls

Silver Spoon MC

The Surgeon

The Heir

The Lawyer

The Prodigy

The Bodyguard

Silver Spoon MC Collection: Nichole's Crew

Echoes of Forever

His Christmas Miracle

Taken by the Hitman

Wicked Saint

<u>The Ruined Trilogy</u>
Physical Science

Wrecked

Wanton

<u>Destination Romance</u>
Romancing the Cowboy

Beach House Beauty

<u>Standalone Titles</u>
A Touch of Summer

Black Velvet

His Secret Obsession

Dirty Boy

Naughty Little Elf

Tempted by December

Devil's Deceit

A Bride for the Beast (writing with Fern Fraser)

<u>Easy on Me</u>
Easy Ride

Easy Surrender

One Night with You

Falling Hard

Model Behavior

Learning Curve

Angel Kisses

Silver Spoon Falls

Xavier's Kitten

Callum's Hope

writing with Loni Ree as Loni Nichole

Dillon's Heart

Razor's Flame

Ryker's Reward

Zane's Rebel

Grizz's Passion (coming soon)

About Nichole Rose

Nichole Rose writes filthy, feel-good romance for curvy readers. Her books feature headstrong, sassy women and the alpha males who consume them. From grumpy detectives to country boys with attitude to instalove and over-the-top declarations, nothing is off-limits.

Nichole is sure to have a steamy, sweet story just right for everyone. She fully believes the world is ugly enough without trying to fit falling in love into a one-size-fits-all box.

When not writing, Nichole enjoys fine wine, cute shoes, and everything supernatural. She is happily married to the love of her life and is a proud mama to the world's most ridiculous fur-babies. She and her husband live in the Pacific Northwest.

You can learn more about Nichole and her books at author nicholerose.com.

f

facebook.com/AuthorNicholeRose/

instagram.com/AuthorNicholeRose

twitter.com/AuthNicholeRose

bookbub.com/authors/nichole-rose

tiktok.com/@authornicholerose